Don't Trust Her

DON'T TRUST HER

ADRIANE LEIGH

JOFFE BOOKS

Joffe Books, London
www.joffebooks.com

First published in Great Britain in 2025

© Adriane Leigh

Cover art by Nick Castle

ISBN: 978-1-83526-955-8

*To women everywhere
doing their best to survive and thrive
in a man's world.
Stand up, speak out, step into your power.
Our daughters need you.*

PROLOGUE

If just one thing had been different, would I still be standing here today?

I've been asking myself that question a lot lately.

And now as I stand here watching you sleep, it's ringing loudly again.

I can't. I can't. I can't do this anymore.

I move closer to the man I love — the man I've always loved.

How could he betray me? He's been living a double life. My father taught me my earliest lessons about what to expect from men — things like trust, loyalty, and honor are fickle — too much to expect from another human. All we have is ourselves. Bile rises as my mother's careless warnings rush through my mind.

Never trust a man. Never trust a man. Never trust a man.

Or a woman, I think.

I was used by all of them, abused and then tossed away. I guess I'm not the first one to be eaten up and spit out by the rich. Betrayal thickens the blood in my veins. Bitterness and wrath chug through my system like a freight train. My mind feels like it's fraying at the edges.

"Look what you made me do, Alex . . ."

CHAPTER ONE

Genevieve

I've never thought much about hell, but it's been on my mind a lot lately. Most of the time I do a pretty fair job of keeping my head above water; making it look like I have everything together is what I do best. But not here. Not now. Hell isn't some faraway place where bad people are sent to suffer for all eternity, hell is right here, in the school pickup lane.

My thoughts wander back to the letter I wrote my husband last night. I wonder if Alexandre has read it yet. I left it sitting on top of the stack of blueprints in his office — maybe he hasn't found it yet. It's been a morning out of the twilight zone and it's taking everything in me to keep it together. I can't expect my husband to drop everything and cater to my needs, even if I secretly wish he would.

"Oh my God — *learn to drive*," I hiss as a white and gold Rolls Royce SUV whips out of the lane without looking and almost sideswipes me. I manage to hit my breaks at the last minute to avoid a fender bender. My nerves have been tightly wound all day, the last thing I'm in the mood for is more people, but it'll only take me a minute to pick up my daughter from school and then I can finally get home and forget this day happened.

I pull into a parking spot and cut the engine. Without looking, I swing my door open wide and nearly knock out a young woman.

"Oh my gosh — I'm so sorry," I apologize. "Are you okay? Are you hurt?"

"No — no," she smiles warmly, "you just got my bag." She pats the oversized canvas tote. "It's saved me from certain death more than a few times." I chuckle at her joke, thankful she's not upset that I nearly just took her out with my car door. Her honey-brown hair falls over one shoulder in loose waves and her eyes are dark and expressive. "Pickup is the craziest part of my day."

"I hear that." I push a hand through my hair. "I just came from — well, it doesn't matter — but it was a terrible day. The last thing I want is to come here and navigate this nightmare."

"You should hire someone to do pickup and drop-off for you. That's what most of the moms here do." She waves her hand at the heel-clad women carrying totes bustling in and out of the school.

"I don't know where I'd find someone to trust to drive my children. I've had help before but it just never works out long. It's so hard to find someone dependable."

"Oh — well, that's what I do, actually." She smiles back at me.

"What? Drive other people's children?" I half-laugh. She's quirky, but I find I kind of like that about her.

"Yeah — I'm an au pair. Official chauffeur is part of the job description. I'm Adeline McKenna." She thrusts out a hand for me to shake. I don't shake it because it seems like an odd gesture, right here in the parking lot at school. "Here—" she digs through her tote and then thrusts a business card at me. "I have plenty of references, I've been doing this since I graduated college. I went to school to be a teacher but I like being an au pair more — less structure and more fulfilling teaching in a home environment."

"And you're available right now? For full-time work, I mean." I take her card and turn it over in my hands. There's a list of three names on the reverse with a phone number for each. References I assume.

"Sure — my last family just moved to Key Biscayne so I've been looking for a new position. As long as it's the right fit, of course." She smiles warmly. "Actually — maybe you know them, their son attended school here before they moved. The Fountains — Katherine and Henry? I just dropped by to return his uniform — Katherine was so busy during the move she forgot to return it"

"Really?" Relief descends on me like a wave. She nods, smile bright. "Katherine and Henry lived in our neighborhood for years." I say by way of an explanation.

Katherine Fountain kept to herself but we often bumped shoulders at the same charity events over the last few years. Truth be told, Alexandre and I could never stand to be around Henry Fountain long — partly because at twenty-five years our senior, we had little in common to talk about and his bigger-than-life personality and brash opinions were hard to hear after more than a minute or two. We used to tease that he was robbing the cradle with Katherine or that he'd finally let her out of her gilded cage for the night and then we'd laugh until we had tears in our eyes when we saw them coming — and take long swallows of whatever cocktail we had in our hands. By the time the Fountains arrived, we were full of giggles. I miss the days when we had inside jokes. And while I never hated the black-tie events filled with Palm Beach's wealthiest and deepest pockets, Alexandre loathed them. And then the minute we found out I was pregnant, the black-tie events were exchanged for decorating the nursery and shopping for breast pumps.

"I have more references—" Adeline digs through her tote bag. She's organized, various vanilla file folders and notebooks

4

are tucked neatly inside. "I usually have a copy with me but it looks like I gave out my last one. My printer ran out of ink and I found out the manufacturer has discontinued my model so I haven't even been able to replace the cartridge—"

"Oh, it's fine. If you worked for Katherine and Henry I don't need to hear anymore." Henry Fountain was the top orthopedic surgeon in the greater Miami area for more than thirty years. When he retired, they sold off their home in Palm Beach and moved permanently to their beach house. I envy them, the chance to start over in a new area with all new faces appeals to me more than I care to admit. "I'll give your references a call when I have time later—"

"I'm afraid the number listed for the Fountains is incorrect though — now that they've moved. The phone number printed on the business card was their landline." She finishes, finally having given up on searching for the full sheet of references she was looking for in that big tote bag. "Oh—" she seems to have remembered something else. "My experience is all right here though." She locates a small stack of papers and thrusts them at me.

"Wow," I say as I thumb through the first few pages. "This looks extensive."

"I also included a few stories — I'm the oldest of five siblings and helped my mom take care of them. I loved it, I still do. I was born to take care of children, my mom always said it comes so naturally to me. There was this one time my little brother almost — well," she stops herself, "you can read about it on page 17 if you want. I also explained a little about my purpose and mission in life and — just some general things." She trails off as if realizing she's talking too much.

I like her already. She reminds me of myself when I was young; driven, dedicated, so eager to please and the fact that she knows Katherine and Henry Fountain instantly puts me at ease.

"This all sounds great. You're the angel I didn't even know I needed. I'll give Katherine a call when I get home but

I'd love to get moving on this — do you think you could come by tonight to meet the children and talk about the job? We're a pretty laid-back family, I think you'll fit right in."

"Yeah — of course. Whatever time you need I can make it work."

"Perfect. Here's my address and cell number." I pass her one of my calling cards. "Would around six tonight be okay?"

Adeline nods. "Six is absolutely perfect."

CHAPTER TWO

Adeline

"It's so hard to get good help — no one wants to work these days." Genevieve Moreau-DuPont, according to the name on her little card, simpers like a spoiled housewife. I've been around more women like her than I care to remember and they're all the same. It takes every ounce of patience in me to smile through the subtle insults and microaggressions. "My husband works all week in Miami. He's the top architect at his firm, they actually pay him a housing stipend to make sure he's nearby all week long. Palm Beach is our dream house, but it's nice to have a little *pied-à-terre* in Miami."

"I bet," I say, taking in the peaked features of her face. She's wearing the same dark pencil skirt paired with Louboutin heels, a string of pearls, lipstick in the same shade as her designer soles, and her soft, brown hair is twisted in a tight chignon that makes her look older than I imagine she is. My gaze hovers over her shoulder. This house is big. Not just big — it's grand and expansive and so modern — it's practically a mansion. Houses like this don't exist in the backwater I come from.

"Oh, forgive me, where are my manners? Come in, come in." Genevieve coos as she opens the front door. Inside and out the home is an elegant shade of white. Ornate black iron balconies rise above the stately pillars that anchor glossy black double doors at the entrance. This house is more mansion than home with rows of perfectly-planted magnolia trees that are just on the cusp of blooming lining the drive. A fountain featuring a life-size heron and alligator sits at the center of the circular drive and a dozen types of palms, hedges, and flowering vines envelop the landscape in lush vegetation.

Inside I find white marble tile meets whitewashed walls as far as the eye can see. The Moreau-DuPont home is a breathtaking open concept on the main floor. I can see a luxury kitchen with glossy black cabinets that match the front entry doors and snow-white marble counter-tops, all accentuated with golden hardware and a golden sink the likes of which I've never seen before. The kitchen is a dramatic design but despite the high-end details, I can't shake the cold and sterile feeling that's seeping into my bones.

"My husband designed our home. I picked out the fixtures and little details, but the rest is all him. His designs always incorporate eco-conscious materials. He's good at what he does, right? That's what makes him the best architect in Miami."

"I've never seen a prettier kitchen," I smile tightly.

"My husband designed a few of the estates in Kensington Bay and he was the lead architect when they designed the community. He's been here since the first day they broke ground, and he picked this piece of land to build our home because it had the best view of the waterway and nature preserve behind the property and it's still walkable to the beach. We spend a lot of nights sipping wine and watching the wildlife at sunset. It's our paradise." Pride swirls in her eyes as envy colors mine.

Kensington Bay Estates is Palm Beach's most exclusive luxury community — every home sits on two acres with pools and tennis courts and a nature preserve anchors the back of the community. I've only seen places like this on HGTV and as the cab driver drove further into the neighborhood, the houses only grew more grand and ostentatious. Circular brick driveways with regal fountains at the center sit sheltered behind ornate iron gates with native wildlife carved into the design. If I had to bet, I'd say each home comes with a price tag in the upper seven figures.

"You have the most beautiful home I've ever seen," I say, honestly.

"Thanks. We've only been here two years. It's so peaceful — Alex and I met in Miami — when we decided we wanted to start a family, Palm Beach just seemed like a natural fit for us. We didn't want to raise children in Miami, so much crime and well, the school system in Palm Beach is one of the best in the state of Florida. Are you from here?"

I shake my head, "Up north, actually."

"Oh, nice. I grew up outside Jacksonville," she offers simply. "So, how about we start with a little tour?" Her smile is bright and her teeth are so artificially white they're blinding. "Let me show you the pool house first — when you come and go we would prefer if you use the side door that the rest of the help uses—"

She continues to ramble but I tune her out. She throws around the term "the help" like it's an indication of class, but really it just makes me cringe. "The help isn't really—"

"Excuse me?" She turns, looking miffed that I've interrupted her house tour.

"Nothing, never mind." I need this job — and more importantly, I *want* it. This position with the DuPonts is the opportunity I've been waiting for — I can't risk it just because I'm offended by this woman's insensitive statements.

"The children's rooms are upstairs along with the theater and playroom. There are a couple other rooms up there that aren't in use — we keep them locked, don't worry about those ones. My husband's office and man cave are in the back of the house — it's the most secluded, near the laundry and guest bedroom. It's out of the way — you won't need to go in there for anything. You already saw the kitchen and the main living area when you came in, and at the end of this hallway," she reaches another door and then pushes it open, "is the staff door."

I suppress an eye roll but my mood instantly lifts when we step out into a tiled pool area. Palm trees shade a beautiful cabana from the spring sunshine on one side, while luxurious lounge chairs line the opposite. This is just the kind of place I can see myself spending all of my free time. I think of long summer days lounging poolside while I watch the wealthy little DuPont brats. The very thought gives me a charge of excitement.

"Albertine swims every day — please keep the back gate locked — there's an inland waterway that runs right through the backyard that is climbing with alligators — one of the neighbors even found one *in* their pool this winter. Albertine refused to swim for weeks." She huffs. "So . . . you'll be the only full-time help — the landscaper and cleaners come a few times a week. You'll meet them over the next few days. My husband, *Alexandre*," she pronounces his full name in a regal French accent that makes my eyes roll, "comes home on Fridays. He works long hours all week so I like to give him his space when he's home. Please, try not to be seen or heard on the weekends. That goes for the children too, if you could be extra attentive when Alexandre is around it will go far to keeping the peace in this house." She chuckles softly as if being told to keep the kids out of sight of their father is a normal request. "He's very nice — my husband — but he's complex. He wasn't raised with a normal family—" she pauses, as if she's rethinking what she's just said. As if she might get in trouble for saying the wrong thing — "Lots of nannies and boarding school and well, neglect I guess. He just . . . doesn't articulate his boundaries well, you see—" she's rambling now — "he just gets impatient when he's tired."

I suppress a huff because it sounds like just the kind of thing a woman says after her husband hits her for the first time.

Genevieve pauses as if lost in thought, sliding her fingertips along the polished string of pearls at her neck. Does she always dress so formal? I've never had a job that required a uniform before, but something about the DuPonts tells me they might be just the type that requires *the help* to look a certain way. Images of *Downton Abbey* come to mind, black-clad maids and buttoned-up butlers making sure the household runs smoothly. I crack a wry smile at the thought — based on her *don't be seen or heard* comment, it certainly sounds like *exactly* what this woman has in mind for *the help*.

She's so polite, so measured, so effortlessly well-contrived. I've come to learn that the crispest collars and most polished pearls often hide the darkest skeletons. People with wealth, prestige, and access have mastered the smokeshow that is a successful life. Private schools, luxury estates, and designer cars are all just part of their theater of distraction.

"Do you have any family in the area?" Genevieve finally thinks to ask.

"No." I draw a fingertip along the mantel of the stone outdoor fireplace.

"Good," she replies quickly. So quickly it almost startles me. I consider asking her exactly *why* that's a good thing, but she continues before I have a chance. I've known this woman for five minutes and already I can tell she likes to hear herself talk. "I'll need you during the week to help with the children while Alexandre is gone, and also on the weekends when he's home. We hardly get any time together anymore, and home isn't exactly restful when there's a crying baby in the house."

I nod. At that very moment, Albertine comes flying down the stairs with a little stuffed puppy in one arm and a beach towel in the other. "Can Puppy and I go swimming, *Maman?*"

I raise an eyebrow as the little girl looks up expectantly at her mother. Genvieve tucks a piece of hair behind her daughter's ear and then answers her in clipped French. The little girl sticks out her tongue at her mother. Genevieve's eyes harden before her daughter's gaze falls in defeat and she turns and climbs the stairs, slowly this time.

"Albertine is fluent in French, Spanish, and of course English. She's learning American Sign Language at school too — she's gifted."

My eyebrows raise. "Is your husband French?"

"He is, but he was born here. He doesn't speak the language as fluently as I do. I worked in Paris for a few years. I was a runway model in my younger years, not that you could tell now." She slides a palm down her face in a tired gesture. "Parenthood really does a number on the body."

"You're so beautiful, you could still be a model," I offer politely.

"You're sweet," she coos but something in her eyes says she doesn't believe me. The truth is, Genevieve is beautiful . . . in a tightly wound Stepford sort of way. "Thirty-four is practically ancient for a supermodel. It's a young woman's game. Oh, and please call me Gen when it's just us — when we're in the presence of others I would prefer if you call me Mrs. Moreau-Dupont."

Again, I have to suppress a laugh. Who does this woman think she is — a fucking Kennedy? Instead of replying, I only nod that I've understood.

"And please — always address my husband as Monsieur Moreau-DuPont. His family is titled in Normandy — Alexandre comes from proper lords and ladies," she giggles like a schoolgirl, "I know that doesn't mean much here, but there . . . who you are is *everything.*"

I don't say anything because she's wrong — at least in part. Who you are in America matters too — only here it's about what side of the tracks you come from more than the last name you were born with. Unless you're an *actual* Kennedy or Rockefeller, in which case, you're modern royalty wherever you go.

I, on the other hand, have been treated like trash since the moment I made my screaming entrance into this world. Being from my tiny inland Florida town will do that to you. A population of less than ten thousand and a median income of not much more than that means that if you're unlucky enough to be born there, you probably won't be leaving. Unless you're me, of course. The day I turned seventeen I left the shithole I called home and never looked back.

You might think being in a mansion like this one, surrounded by wealth and prestige, would leave me feeling like a fish out of water, but in fact, it's the opposite. I've been crawling my way out of the gutter for a decade waiting for such a time as this.

I'll be right at home in Genevieve Moreau-DuPont's life because I was born to be here.

CHAPTER THREE

Genevieve

"I'd like to plan something special, but I need your help." I approach Adeline on Friday morning. She's been here just one night and already she seems to have made herself right at home. She gives me a dubious look, so I continue. "Nothing too big, just a nice candlelit dinner, maybe Alexandre's favorite French dish. Do you know how to make *coq au vin*?"

Adeline gives me a puzzled look. "I've heard of it . . . I've never made it."

"Oh, it's so easy. I would do it but I have lunch with the other wives in an hour so I don't have the time. I'll send you a link to a recipe to use — you don't mind, right? I have chicken and a beautiful red wine — you won't even have to go to the store." Adeline doesn't reply, almost like she's confused by my request. I was really hoping this one would be the right fit, but I'm finding her a little lackluster in the kitchen. "Are you okay?"

"I'm great," her face brightens, "just a little overwhelmed at the thought of making a fancy French dish. I'm not really a great cook."

"Oh there's nothing to it; quality ingredients and some patience are the only secret. So obviously Laurent doesn't go to daycare on Fridays; don't forget to pick Albertine up at three from school; and if you could keep the children upstairs during dinner that would be great. Alexandre is usually home around four on Fridays."

"Oh. Sure." Adeline jostles the baby on one hip. My boy's little dark curls are still wild from his nap and I smile as I tuck a lock behind his ear. He swipes at my finger and grasps it tightly, pulling it to his mouth to suck on one knuckle.

"He's teething right now, *mon petit choux*," I whisper. His toothless grin turns wide before he tries to yank my finger back into his mouth. "I've been trying to speak to him in French as much as possible — Albertine's first word was *maman* — the word from mummy — isn't that so sweet? This little guy is already a rebel though, everything about him is different from our little girl. He's loud and crazy and even started crawling and walking early — he has no fear. From the moment Laurent came into this world he's been moving at a hundred miles an hour and it takes everything in me to keep up with him."

"He has big boy energy, huh?" Adeline grins and tickles my son under his chubby little chin. He giggles outrageously and for the first time I think maybe she'll be the perfect fit for our family. Maybe she's just what we need right now; she certainly is saving my life by showing up for this job at a moment's notice.

I'm not sure what Alexandre will have to say about me hiring a stranger off the street to take care of our children, but without him here all week to help, I've been drowning. So I really can't be bothered to worry about what he might think about Adeline.

To me, she is perfect.

CHAPTER FOUR

Adeline

Alexandre Moreau-DuPont arrived home exactly at four o'clock today just as Genevieve said he would, but I have not yet seen the man of the house. He keeps to himself, I'll give him that. No wonder Genevieve told me to make sure the kids aren't seen or heard . . . because he is practically a ghost in his own home. I caught a glimpse of him on my way out to the pool house a few minutes ago but he seemed too lost in his own world to even see me.

That is until Albertine streaks across the patio with two pool noodles tucked under her arms and jumps feet first into the deep end.

I rush to the side of the pool on instinct, but then remember that Albertine is a strong swimmer. The little girl surfaces across the pool and calls to her daddy. When I finally look up, he's sitting on the edge of the lounger, legs spread wide and hands clasped between his knees.

And he's looking directly at me.

His dark hair is cropped short, his skin a warm shade of honey, as if he spends all of his free time in the Florida sunshine. He's probably the kind of man that spends weekends at the golf club sipping gin and tonics and networking. He's handsome by any standard and I'm surprised to find he looks younger than his wife.

I gulp down strange feelings. A heady mix of desire and anxiety swim in my stomach as our gazes remain locked. He looks . . . *sad.* This is not at all what I expected. Maybe he's uncomfortable with his wife hiring someone else to watch their children — that's usually the issue most husbands have about these situations.

Albertine shouts and splashes water in the direction of her father to get his attention. It works, because he finally tears his gaze from mine and shoots a startling smile her way. I can't hear what they're saying but a moment later she climbs out of the pool and runs into his lap. He laughs, points out that she's gotten all of his clothes soaking wet, but then he kisses her forehead and lifts her into his arms. Her little arms and legs flail as she squeals and giggles, then he tosses her into the pool as she screams with glee.

They have a good relationship, I can tell. I fight down a bite of pain as I think about my own father. If he'd been half the father that Alex seems to be, well, who knows where I'd be then.

I breathe a sigh of exhaustion, giving the two of them space while I return to the kitchen to clean up dinner. I spend the next twenty minutes washing the dishes that I used to slow simmer the *coq au vin* all afternoon. I don't know if I pulled off the recipe because I've never had *coq au vin* before and because the dinner was meant to be romantic between Genevieve and Alexandre, I didn't get a chance to try it. Not even a bite. Based on the amount of leftovers, though, it would seem I did *not* knock it out of the park. Next time I'll just place a takeout order from the French restaurant in downtown Palm Beach. Genevieve can judge me all she wants, but at least I wouldn't have to waste my time making food that no one is going to eat. Genevieve is one of those overachieving moms. I can tell because the freezer is overflowing with healthy pre-made and perfectly-portioned meals for the kids.

I dry my hands with a clean dish towel and then hang it on the oven handle before sucking in a deep breath. Genevieve has run me so ragged today I haven't even had a chance to settle into the pool house. Apparently it was a silly notion to think I might have enough time to lounge by the pool at lunch or in the evenings before bed.

I've been here for twenty-four hours and already I can tell there will be no lounging at the Moreau-DuPont estate.

I move through the darkened house on light footsteps, careful to be neither seen or heard as Genevieve requested. It's just after nine o'clock and it feels like I've been dragging for a week. I'm not used to my work days being from sunup to sunset, but I like being busy. If my days weren't filled with things to do, I'd be pulling my hair out. A yawn escapes before I can catch it as I flip the kitchen light off and then make my way down the long, polished hall to the back door. I open it quietly, taking in the moonlight reflecting off the pool.

A quiet sob fills the night air.

"Ms.?" I say into the dim light.

"Oh — I didn't know anyone was out here." Genevieve sniffles and then turns in a lounger to face me. "Come. Sit."

I do as she asks, only because I don't know what else to do.

"The *coq au vin* was wonderful. Thank you for putting so much time and effort into making dinner perfect."

"You're welcome," I utter.

"Do you like it here?" She blurts.

"S-sure," I say, surprised by her question. "I've only been here a day — what's not to like?"

"Me. My husband. The children. Take your pick." She pours wine into an empty glass and passes it to me. "Drink. It's not like Alexandre will be having any." Another sad sigh falls off her lips. "It's a vintage Bordeaux we picked up in the South of France two summers ago. The vintner's best bottle."

"Thank you." I accept the wine and then take the barest of sips. "It's good."

She smiles. "It should be for seven hundred dollars."

I nearly spit out my next sip. I've never had anything in my mouth that costs this much. Is this what seven-hundred-dollar wine is supposed to taste like? Because all I can taste is a flavor so bitter I have to suppress a cringe. I set the glass on the table between us. "Your husband didn't enjoy dinner?"

"Oh, I don't know that he *didn't* enjoy it. I guess I don't know if he enjoyed it either. Even after you get to know him, he's a pretty reticent person. What you see is what you get — work, eat, sleep, repeat. Everything changed when he was offered a chance at being a partner at the firm. I knew it would be hard raising children while my husband spends most of the week in Miami, but I didn't expect him to be so . . . checked out even when he's home." She turns her gaze up to puffs of clouds over our head that are lit with silver moonlight. "Men — can't live with them, can't live without them, right?"

I crack a sideways grin, not because I know anything about living with men — but because it's what's expected after a statement like that. Genevieve and Alexandre Moreau-DuPont have a beautiful life but some sort of sadness simmers just beneath the surface of this woman.

"Did your life turn out like you expected?" Genevieve's question pierces the silence.

"I . . ." I take another sip of the terrible Bordeaux because this is a big question for my first full day on the job. "I don't know. Maybe?"

She huffs. "Nothing has turned out like I expected. *Nothing.* From John Paul Gautier and Alexander McQueen shows to shitty diapers and PTA meetings. I walked the runway for Tom Ford when he was at Gucci." I swear I hear tears in her voice before she drains the rest of her wine glass and then pours another. "It's funny, when you're on top of the world you don't realize that the only place to go from there is down." Her frown deepens. "I knew the runway shows wouldn't last forever, but I had this silly idea that I could transition into ad campaigns or maybe put my name on a make-up brand. I don't know what I thought, but I can tell you that I did not imagine a world of freezer meals and cloth diapers."

"The children are so sweet and happy, you've obviously done a wonderful job—"

She laughs. "For what? Just to have them leave me when they turn eighteen? Tell me they hate me and send me their therapy bills to prove it? I know how this goes. Motherhood is the most fulfilling and thankless job on the planet. *So they say*. Can I tell you a secret?" She leans closer, like a teenager confessing a crush on a boy, "I'm still waiting for the fulfilling part to kick in."

My eyebrows lift at her admission. I've known this woman for just over twenty-four hours and already she's admitting to the things that most people spend a lifetime burying. I find I'm liking her more than I thought I would.

"Such is life, I guess," she continues. "I'm thankful I made enough in the modeling years to be sitting here today, next to the heated pool and commiserating over my miserable life with the help."

And there it is. The micro-insult I should have known was coming. The reminder that this woman and I will never be friends. We are too different. We will always be too different. To her, I will always be nothing more than the help.

CHAPTER FIVE

Genevieve

"It's a funny feeling — the sense of fitting in and yet still being an outcast," I say as I press on the skin of a tomato to test its ripeness. After dropping the children off at school, we came here, to my favorite organic market for groceries.

"What do you mean, Ms.?" Adeline answers politely.

"Oh, please. I told you, call me Gen when it's just us. No need for fussy formalities at the market." Adeline nods, dusting her fingertips along the rinds of a basket of avocados. "We should have tacos tonight. My parents always did taco Tuesday when I was a kid — Albertine will love making her own tacos. Let's make guacamole too." I pluck four ripe avocados from the basket. "Should we do chicken or beef?"

Adeline doesn't answer, as if she's lost in her own thoughts. Or maybe she's just ignoring me.

"Oh, no. Not *her,*" I whisper.

"*Who?*" Adeline chirps.

"It's one of the other wives. She goes to my mommy group and her daughter is in the same class as Albertine. She's the perfect example of what I mean about *not* fitting in," I admit. "We look the same, we live the same lifestyle, we attend the same parties and charity events . . . but making conversation with the other wives feels like talking to aliens. I don't know if it's me or them." We continue down the aisle as I consider exactly what it is about the other chic mommies that makes me feel so out of place. "Most women are so bitchy — living in the model apartments when I was young was another level of hell. Catty backstabbing and mood swings . . . even the nice ones hide who they really are and it's no different now. The other wives play nice but once they see the luxury estate and vintage Chanel in my closet the dynamic always shifts. And once the green-eyed monster arrives there's no getting rid of it, ya know? My friendships always fizzle fast after that."

"Genevieve! It's so lovely to see you!" Marissa, the other wife I'd been trying to avoid, has just turned into our aisle.

"Hi, Marissa." I shuffle the basket on my arm as her gaze travels up and down my form. "How are you?"

"Oh, ya know, the same as usual. Michael is in London for a few weeks on business so I've been juggling the kids and the staff and everything else. You weren't at that school board meeting a few nights ago but things got heated — apparently some parents are taking issue with the pledge donations and then someone stood and pointed out that the current chair of the board has been carrying on with the treasurer — you know how it is in Palm Beach, honey, everyone has a secret." She stops to scan me up and down and then I swear I see a look of pity cross her face, "Forgive me, dear, I should have asked — how are you doing?"

"I'm sorry, Marissa — I have so much on my plate today and Alexandre is only home today and tomorrow so I hate to linger . . ." I shoot her a weak smile.

"Oh sure, sure. Listen, let's get together this week. I'll call up the other wives and we'll have a pool party with the kids — how does that sound?" Her pearly smile widens.

I don't reply to her, only give an apologetic nod and then press a palm at Adeline's elbow to direct us away from Marissa and her school board drama. Once we're out of earshot I lean close and murmur, "There's a reason I don't go to those school board meetings. Marissa Aston is the ex-wife of a Hollywood executive producer. He had a second family with the maid and she made off with half his money. She remarried richer and older and they settled in Palm Beach last summer. She's sweet, but you can't trust her. You can't trust any of them."

Adeline smiles as she shoves a bunch of cilantro to her nose and inhales. "Yeah?"

"Drama. Drama. Drama. It's just posturing anyway — who brings a Birkin to PTA meetings? It's trashy if you ask me." Adeline doesn't reply, so I continue. "You're so easy to talk to — I'm so glad we met. It was pure serendipity that you found me just when I needed you the most."

"You're sweet, Ms. — I mean Gen." She says, her smile warm as she peers back at me over the bunch of cilantro. I realize I never asked her her age — I guess I just assumed she was within a few years of my own thirty-four years, but as I look at her now I see the plumpness of youth in her cheeks and a naive sparkle in her dark irises. She reminds me of the girl I used to be: beautiful in a natural, make-up-free sort of a way. A twinge of jealousy sparks to life when I think about all the Botox and filler it takes to keep me from looking so exhausted all the time.

Adeline did her job well last night — she prepared our romantic meal right under his nose without ever being seen. It's not hard to do — Alexandre lives and dies by his routine. The first thing he does when he arrives home every Friday afternoon is give our children a kiss on their foreheads, then showers, works in his office until dinner, and then retires to his den before bed. Sometimes he takes meetings or reads the latest *Architectural Digest*. Whatever he does, he does in private. I understand his need for privacy because he spends all week in the office with people — some wives might expect their husband to sacrifice his time all weekend in service to their family but I'm not one of them. I understand his drive to achieve — just like his father, he works until his mind can no longer function. To say he's a workaholic would be an understatement, but it's one of the things that made me fall head over heels for him all those years ago. He had his career and I had mine.

Until we had children.

Now he has his career.

And I have nothing.

CHAPTER SIX

"Ms. Durden?" The caller says over the phone line as I tuck a stack of bills into my wallet.

"This is her." I take a bite out of a room-service croissant. I'm still wearing last night's little black dress and can only find one black stiletto. I bend, hunting for the heel under the hotel bed.

The caller continues. "Next of kin to Ty Durden?"

I groan. "What did he do now?"

"He's been admitted to Trinity Medical Hospital downtown. His liver is failing. I imagine this isn't your first rodeo with him?"

"Hardly," I grit. "Is he in a coma again?" The last time I saw him he was in a coma too. I prefer him that way, our visits are more peaceful.

"Yes, we've placed him in a medically-induced coma." The doctor informs me.

"Thank you for calling," I say before hanging up the phone.

I blink away my annoyance as I recall the last time we were in this place. My father, dying on the floor in front of me, while I cradle his head and beg him to stay with me until the ambulance arrives. He made it that time. Now I mostly wish he hadn't. I thought I could save him then, but you can't save someone from themselves. In fact, I should have poisoned him when I had the chance and put him out of his misery then. Life would certainly have been easier if I had.

After ten minutes of gurgling and having a seizure on the floor, paramedics arrived and I rode with my father in the back, holding his hand as personnel pumped him full of medications to save him from the vodka that he's poisoned his body with every day. I knew then that ambulance ride would be the last ride we'd ever take together. I vowed never to pick up one of his phone calls again. I vowed I would leave this man and all the abusive heartache he left me struggling to heal from in the past.

I was seventeen when I walked out of his life and never looked back. It doesn't keep him from trying to reel me back into the shitstorm though.

A text message lights up my screen then. Everything go well last night?

I hiss with annoyance, finding the missing heel and then sitting back on my bottom to reply to the text message.

All went well. He's a good one. Mentioned flying me to Europe for a job.

LOL comes the reply. He tells all of them that, don't get your hopes up.

I don't reply to that. I've been working with Hugo, as he prefers to be called, for almost five years. It's true that I've heard lots of false promises in the moment, but something about this guy tells me he could be the real deal. He's a kind and well-connected venture capitalist in the fashion industry, not just in Miami but in Europe and Asia too. And he always requests me specifically when he's in town. I find after all these years it's easier on me to just emotionally invest in one or two of the men at a time, always the most successful ones that could get me a little further away from the gutter. I don't have any talents beyond appealing to men. That's the gift dear old dad left me with: how to play a toxic man until he's eating out of your hand and begging for more.

I could compartmentalize at first, let my vision seep to black just as their greedy hands began roaming my skin. But the more aggressive the men got, the harder it became to slip into another world. Spitting and choking were just the beginning. Soon the requests grew darker, more involved — they actually expected me to act like I'm enjoying it. I think back on the day that Hugo approached me on the sidewalk in Palm Beach. I'd only been at the women's shelter for two days, fresh from

Pahokee and still swaddled in innocence, when he offered me a job at his elite estate massaging clients and hosting elegant parties. I was seventeen and so desperate for a job I didn't ask questions. But it doesn't matter. Even if I'd known what I was getting into, I still would have done it. I didn't have a choice. Opportunity doesn't look the same to everyone, and for a girl from the sticks, a man offering a job massaging wealthy men is an opportunity not to be missed.

It was never just massaging of course. Silly me.

But the tips are good. Sometimes even surpassing an entire month of my parent's salary in one evening alone. And the more I connected with the men, the more I made them feel validated and heard and nurtured in ways they'd never been by their wives. The more I cater to their needs, the more attached they get. I bought my first car last month thanks to Henry and his fifty-thousand-dollar birthday present. I may live paycheck to paycheck a lot of the time, but at least I have a Porsche Cayenne to call my own. But I don't want to cater to these men forever. I want a life for myself outside of clients and little black dresses and designer lingerie. I want to be a part of Palm Beach society, not just on the outside looking in.

A knock sounds at the door then. "Housekeeping."

"Give me a minute, please!" I call back, shoving my heels on my feet. I pause at the wall of windows that overlook downtown Miami and the bay beyond. Wealth and luxury as far as the eye can see. A world away from Pahokee.

I sigh. I'll have to work at least another two years taking every client Hugo offers and catering to all of their depraved needs to even hope to earn enough to buy my own home. Growing up in Pahokee's finest mobile home community leaves much to be desired.

"I could use another opportunity about now."

I think how my life would have turned out if I'd followed the path set for me. There were two options for a girl from Pahokee: go to college and earn your way out with your brain, or stay and have babies and collect child support payments to make ends meet. Neither felt good enough — sure spending four years in college would have granted me access to plenty of eligible bachelors from plenty of good families, but how could I earn my keep?

In truth, I never did have a plan the night I walked out of Pahokee. I only knew that I would never look back. Looking back would only slow me down. Accepting the guilt my father threw at me — the expectation to be not just his daughter but his caregiver, his companion, even his financial security — would have been a death sentence for my dreams. People like my parents don't invest in emotional attachments, they believe that blood is thicker than water and that it comes with the obligation to show up no matter the circumstance just because we share genes. This same sense of familial obligation didn't apply to me though — they weren't required to show up when I was a kid, hungry for food and stability and love.

Leaving Pahokee and my family behind saved my life, even if it meant spending time in strange beds with strange men. Begging the cab company to drive the hour out to Pahokee to pick me up and bring me into Palm Beach on my seventeenth birthday cost me all that I had. And it was the best $300 I've ever spent. The taxi driver didn't know it then, but he was delivering me from hell one mile at a time.

And by the time we arrived in Palm Beach, I was a new woman.

A proud smile turns my cheeks as I glance down at my phone, finding the list of Miami's most successful bachelors that I've been adding to over the weeks.

Alexandre Moreau-DuPont - Architect - Trinity Medical Hospital *is at the top of my list.*

This is perfect. Like the universe has aligned. A two birds one stone kind of situation. I'll visit my nearly dead dad and just happen to bump into one of Miami's hottest up-and-coming architects. I love when a plan comes together.

A cheerful grin slides over my lips. "I can't wait to meet you, Alexandre Moreau-DuPont."

CHAPTER SEVEN

Adeline

"Gen — you hired a nanny without talking to me? I swear I don't know who you are anymore." I hear Alexandre Moreau-DuPont's voice before I've even met him officially. "Where did you find her? You can't just adopt people off the street like homeless puppies."

My heart sinks at the annoyance lacing his words. He definitely does not appreciate that his wife has hired me without consulting him first. I can't imagine why, she's the one that's home with the kids all week, not him.

He's right to be concerned though. I'm not what I've led her to believe. But what's the harm in a few white lies if they help me get from A to Z? It's not like he'll remember me anyway. It's been years since the last time we met and I look like a different person now. I've made sure of that. There was a moment at the pool yesterday when I thought I might have seen a flicker of recognition in his eyes, but it's impossible — it's been too long and I'm not the same girl I was when he knew me last.

At that moment, Albertine throws a foam noodle into the pool and then launches herself onto it with a shriek that splits my eardrums. I half-chuckle as I think about getting ear plugs for this job, but then, I wouldn't be able to eavesdrop from a pool lounger on Genevieve and her husband.

"Alexandre — she worked for Henry and Katherine Fountain. You know Katherine would never have someone in their house she didn't trust implicitly." Gen's tone is soft and measured. She's different with him — I don't need to see them together to know that. It's funny listening to someone talk about how fake people can be only to watch her turn around and slide a superficial smile on her face when her husband arrives.

"Please — you never know what kind of crazies are out there. We've talked about this, I know we have." His tone is dismissive. No wonder her energy shifts at the mention of him. I don't think I like the Gen that shows up when he's around — he brings out something in her that leaves a rotten pit in my stomach. "But Henry probably ran at least a half a dozen background checks on her . . ." His voice is lower, more understanding. "I'm sure she's fine, I'm sorry for getting upset."

Was he like that when I knew him? I hardly remember. Maybe I've blocked it out.

"Watch me jump!" Albertine calls from the pool edge. I glance her way and give a small wave. She waves back wildly and then poises herself to dive head first.

My heart lodges in my throat and prevents the scream of warning that I should be directing at her right now. Albertine is an impeccable swimmer, but she still needs supervision in the event of an accident. Before I can say anything, she's diving head first into the shallow end of the pool. I find my voice, yelling her name once before launching out of the lounger and across the patio to where she vanished. I can't see her. Am I too late? Did she already sink to the bottom of the pool like a bag of bricks?

"Albertine!" I call, eyes searching the clear water.

"Haha! Scared you!" Albertine pops her towhead out of the water at the opposite end of the pool.

"Albertine, please don't do that again." I hold a palm to my hammering heart.

"Scaredy cat, scaredy cat! You look so funny!" Albertine taunts me and it's the first time I think I actually don't like this little girl. She's spoiled and reckless and I really don't have the patience for it.

"Adeline, *mon petit* — what's all the ruckus out here?" Gen is hovering at my shoulder.

"*Maman!* Watch me jump!" Adeline squeals as she rushes to pull herself out of the pool.

"She's a wild one," I gripe.

"She is." Gen's eyes cut up to the window that her and her husband were just arguing from. I assume it's their primary bedroom, but I haven't been to that wing of the house to know. Gen's house tour only included one wing of the top floor — where the children sleep. Albertine's room is large — larger than any bedroom I've ever slept in. Because both twin beds were unmade this morning when I helped dress Albertine for the day, I assume Gen is sleeping in her daughter's bedroom at night and not with her husband.

All is not as calm in paradise as Gen would have it seem.

"Listen — I know it's a lot to ask but can you try harder to keep her quiet while Alexandre is home? He gets migraines and just can't tolerate the loud noise of the children."

"Yeah — sure, sure. I'm sorry," I sputter.

"Albertine — love, why don't you come in and get ready for bed? The sun will be down soon. It will give us just enough time for a bath and a bedtime story." Gen leans into me and lowers her tone. "You don't mind doing bath and bedtime tonight, do you?"

I shake my head. "No, Ms."

She nods, a satisfied smile crossing her face. "Perfect. You're a godsend. I don't know what I would do without you." *Run a bath and read a book to your kid* is what I'm thinking, but instead I only nod. She turns and heads back into the house on quick strides. "Oh, Adeline?" She calls over her

31

shoulder as she reaches the door, "Please make sure you have the baby monitor — if Laurent wakes up in the middle of the night I don't want him to disturb Alexandre."

I nod, already suppressing a yawn. It's been a long day, from dawn to dusk and still going. It's not clear to me how Genevieve spent her day — after the market she disappeared into her room and never came back out. I was left with the kids and the meal prep and the cleaning, and now the bedtime routine too. On top of being called the help all the time, I'm starting to feel like a second-class citizen.

I don't get paid nearly enough for this job. I'm not just taking care of the kids — I'm taking care of the parents too — and all in a home where sadness splinters the air and madness brews just beneath the surface. Gen owes me more than a salary, she owes me everything.

CHAPTER EIGHT

Genevieve

"Did you hear about Addison Hillsong?" Fawn cradles a tea-cup in one hand as she leans into the other wives gathered around the pool.

"No. What?" Marissa's eyes widen as she swishes her bare legs back and forth in the warm pool water. The children are playing just out of earshot of today's neighborhood gossip.

"Apparently Dennis came home early on her birthday to surprise her and found her and her tennis coach . . . in an intimate entanglement." Fawn's eyes glimmer as she reveals this last part.

"Addison and Maxim? No." Marissa's eyes widen.

Fawn nods. "I just found out at the school board meeting last night. Isn't it crazy? He's so young."

"Maxim is twenty-five — plenty old enough," Juanita flicks her wrist with a saucy glint in her dark eyes. "I bet he's a *very* thorough and energetic instructor."

"Oh! Speaking of the school board meeting—" Marissa shifts the conversation, "did you hear that the VanAllens are threatening to pull their endowment pledge if the head of the school board doesn't step down?"

"No — why?" Fawn breathes. I can't for the life of me bring myself to care about any of this. It's like watching an episode of *Real Housewives of Palm Beach* unfold in real-time. I've never been into reality tv so it's ironic that I seem to have found myself living inside a trashy one. These women are a different breed than me — they're all East coast class and breeding and the farthest thing from my own upbringing.

The women continue to prattle on as I do my best to tune them out. Albertine is playing a mermaid game with Francine, Fawn's daughter, and they're both giggling and whispering in the sweetest way. Like little Palm Beach housewives in the making. A split-second of disdain crawls through me as I realize Albertine is destined to grow up to be one of them — a spoiled childhood in a gated community where class and manners matter less than the size of the bank account. Would it serve Albertine better to grow up in the real world? Away from superficial, bored, and pretentious women that hook up with their tennis coaches?

I crack a smile then when I realize it isn't far off from the real world really — this is just the Palm Beach version of events. The world is filled with bored, superficial, pretentious people — the more adept she is at navigating it the better off she'll be. Let her swim with sharks in the water, I think, it's a skill that will serve her later in life. And at least here in Palm Beach she'll be well-connected.

"Gen—" Fawn bumps my shoulder to get my attention — "is there any more cannabis tea?"

"Sure—" I stand to go get some but she stops me.

"Oh, I don't want anymore — just that little bit already has my head feeling loopy," she giggles like a teenager, "I'd love to bring some home to Jerry though."

"Definitely." A fake smile covers my face. It's funny how I call these women friends but the only way I can stand to sit with them is if we're not sober.

I sigh, adjusting the top of my swimsuit, thinking about when Alex and I first moved into this house. We spent countless late nights swimming naked in the pool, drunk on champagne and first love. He was my everything then, not anymore though. I'd have to see him once in a while for that to happen. It hurts to be strangers with someone who used to be your everything. Maybe Alex working away all week is only a phase, maybe if he makes partner he can take long weekends or — I stop myself from this train of thought. I can't keep living in the future, hoping, hoping, hoping for more from him and only getting less and less.

"I'll never understand these women that let anyone under the age of sixty into their homes with their husbands — men are simple, put fresh meat in front of them and you know how it goes." She waves. "Fucking the help is a fantasy for them."

"And apparently for Addison too," Fawn quips.

"I bet it's not the first time she's done this," Juanita says.

"I heard they have an open *arrangement*," Fawn whispers.

"Please. Half the people in this neighborhood do." Marissa sips her tea languidly.

"I wonder how long it's been going on—" Fawn muses, then looks over at me. "Wait, didn't you say you just hired a new nanny? I hope she's not pretty." Fawn chuckles.

I repress a frown in favor of a tight smile. "I did. Only for a little help here and there — I trust Alexandre. He's not home all week anyway so I doubt they'll even run into each other. I just needed a little help with the day-to-day things right now."

Fawn's gaze remains trained on mine. "Sure, honey, of course you do."

Marissa smiles at me, eyes warm and genuine. "You know if you ever need anything, we're here for you. We're only ever a phone call away." She pats my knee. An icy chill slides through my system with her touch.

Her false sense of pity makes me want to vomit into her teacup.

I don't want pity from any of these women.

* * *

"Would you like me to prepare lunch, Ms.?" Adeline appears from behind my shoulder. I'm camped out in the living room on the white leather sectional a few hours later and *Gilmore Girls* is playing on Netflix but I'm not paying any attention. I've seen every episode at least three times, just the sound of Rory and Lorelai's voices calm me on days like today.

Days when regret infects my system like a virus.

"No, thank you, Adeline. Alexandre already left for Miami, anyway." I pat the soft, leather sofa at my side. "Do you like *Gilmore Girls*?"

"I've never watched it." Adeline settles on the cushion and shifts, like she doesn't belong. Maybe she doesn't. But I'm not sure I do either.

"It's my favorite to watch on bad days." I take another sip of my mimosa. "Actually, could you top me off? The orange juice is in the door of the fridge."

Adeline stands from the sofa and moves silently in the kitchen behind me. She's so good at not being seen *or heard*, it's almost eerie. It's like living with a phantom in my own house — only one that cleans and cooks and keeps the children quiet.

"Do you have bad days a lot, Ms.?" Adeline inquires as she pours a splash of orange juice in my flute and then adds a generous pour of champagne.

"More lately, I guess. I think it's just exhaustion. Trying to be supermom comes with a price, I guess." I swallow half of my glass and then swirl the rest of the contents as I watch the bubbles fizz and evaporate to nothing. "I used to sip my mimosas on the rooftops of Paris and Milan dripping in designer fashion with the most fabulous movers and shakers in the world — celebrities and yachts and summers in Ibiza were the norm. Now? Now I sip my Sunday morning mimosas in pajamas that smell like baby puke. What a glamorous life I lead, right?" She huffs. "Thinking about who I was then compared to now gives me whiplash."

Adeline doesn't say anything. I'm not really sure there's anything to be said, but it feels good to finally have someone to talk to about these things. The other wives seem to have taken to motherhood so effortlessly, I envy them. I thought I was them, but what do you do when it takes having something to realize you don't want it? For a while now I've been feeling like there is a void in my chest where my maternal instincts would fit neatly.

"Do you want children, Adeline?" I finally ask.

"I haven't really thought about it." She shifts on the cushion next to me, her eyes darting around the room as if just being in my home is uncomfortable for her.

"I've done my best to make this big fucking house a home but I swear it's impossible," I complain. She doesn't reply, so I continue. "Everyone thinks a big house is the dream, but it's a nightmare. I can't keep up with the cleaning — Albertine has practically ruined this Italian leather sofa. It shipped directly from Milan and took eight months to arrive . . . all for a five-year-old to jump on it and stain it and have accidents, ugh — everything is such a chore with that one and no one I've hired to clean this house can do a job that's up to Alexandre's standards. I don't blame him for wanting things a certain way — he's very particular and I know just how he likes everything. I can practically read his mind at this point — but . . ." I sip my mimosa and sigh, "fitting into this good little wife mold is exhausting." I let my thoughts linger as Lorelai and Luke talk about something on the screen. "Sometimes I wonder if fitting into the good wife mold is killing me slowly." I finish my mimosa and then mix another for myself. "I *never* get help from Alexandre. He was always so attentive and loving before the children were born but now . . . it's like we cease to exist. I can't help but wonder what it would have been like to raise children with someone who actually cared to be a father." I sip and sigh, then crack a rueful grin because sipping and sighing has been about all I've been doing lately. "I'm sorry for unloading so much on you — you're just so easy to talk to. I feel like I can really unplug with you in a way I can't with the other wives or even Alexandre. I'm so grateful to have you, Adeline. The way you're always one step ahead of me is priceless — like having another me in the house. Alexandre just doesn't get it."

CHAPTER NINE

"Miss." The doctor shuffles a patient chart in his hands. "Your father is lucky to be alive. His liver is operating at five per cent functionality — if his neighbor would have found him even an hour later, I don't think he'd still be with us."

I sob softly and whisper a thanks to him. The doctor leaves me standing in the hallway outside of my father's room. He's been in an induced coma for twelve hours while doctors work to undo the damage he's done to himself.

I hug my bag close to my chest as I walk in the direction of the elevators swearing that I will never see this man again. He's poisoned his own body, along with my childhood, and every relationship I've ever had since. Just seeing his face again brings back a rush of pain. My stomach burns and twists as I think about all we've been through together. The bond I share with my parents is built on shared trauma. For years I held my breath, hoping the day would come that it would occur to them all that they're missing out on — me. I was not to be seen or heard, so I spent my childhood hiding. And I hid so well I never even found myself. Under a constant cloud of criticism and addiction, I grew into someone with the superpower of adaptation. My needs, boundaries and personality just malleable enough to suit the ever-shifting moods of the house.

I glance down to the slash of a white scar on my wrist. I grit my teeth until pain radiates through my jaw as I recall the night I climbed through my bedroom window and a shard of bent metal sliced my tender flesh. I was twelve and spent most of the night at a party with my other classmates. My father was passed out on the couch when I left before dinner so I'd left him a sticky note on his 6-pack in the fridge. The first place he'd stumble once he slept off his hangover would be the fridge to start his drinking again. But apparently he didn't that night, because when I crawled through the window just after midnight, he was sitting on my bed. Waiting. Smoking a cigarette. Smirking with the promise of my punishment.

My father relished these moments. I think because I worked so hard to be not seen or heard, on the rare opportunity that I fucked up, my punishment felt like his reward. And this night was no different. First he demanded to know where I was. When I told him he cackled, passed me his open Miller Lite and lit cigarette, and told me I was only allowed to party with him. I explained that it wasn't that kind of party — this was just kids from school having a pool party that ran late — but he was convinced that his worst fears of me were reality.

And so, the first time I got drunk was with my father while my wrist bled out on my bedroom carpet.

I wrapped my wrist in a hand towel and then guzzled three disgusting beers as my father yelled about raising a foolish, fuck-up of a daughter. Red-faced and raging, he stalked around the house like a caged animal, lit cigarettes, puffing on them once or twice, then setting them in the nearest ashtray, distracted as he moved through the rooms looking for somewhere else to focus his anger. The cigarettes burned out slowly, the ashy remains wasted, just like my potential.

Well, who has the last laugh now, Dad?

As I fill my bank account with cash and opportunity, he dies out in a hospital bed, an ashy fading husk of a human just like those wasted cigarettes.

The smell of beer still makes my stomach lurch all of these years later. From that day forward, I promised I would never put something in my body that would steal my focus. No chemical was worth risking my future. I'd needed to remain sharp and calculating if I had any hope of surviving outside of Pahokee.

But that left me with only one option.

I'd need to work harder and smarter than both of my parents combined. I was smart enough to see that their dead-end jobs never got them out of the gutter, and out of the gutter was the only place I wanted to be. The very next day, I offered to write an English essay for my best friend. She paid me $5 and my first business was born. Six months later, with my savings growing at too small a pace, I let one of the varsity football players feel me up for $20. I have no shame, how could I? Compartmentalizing my pain while men used me was my superpower. I did what I had to and I saved every damn dime. There were many nights that Dad's dinner budget went to Miller Lite so I dug out of my savings for tv dinners or frozen pizza. In those last few years with him I mastered the art of acting. I evolved into a shapeshifter, becoming what anyone else needed to achieve my greater goals. Survival was the name of my game. And for the first time, with the goal of escaping Pahokee close enough to taste, I found myself.

I jerk back to reality as the elevator doors slide open and I walk through the lobby and into the Miami heat. And right into a stranger.

"Woah—" heavy palms steady me at the waist, "Sorry about that."

I look up through my watery gaze. Rich brown eyes lined in thick lashes stare down at me. "S-sorry."

"Oh — here — sit." He guides me to a stone bench and settles me on it. He bends at the knee, hands anchoring the bench on either side of me. "Can I get you anything?"

I shake my head, more tears flooding my eyes. He's handsome in the sort of way that takes my breath away. Concern swims in his irises and sends tingles spiraling through me. I finally say, "I just lost my father."

"Oh." His eyes are warm and brown. Trusting. "I'm so sorry."

"It's okay — I just need to get myself in a cab and get home. I haven't been able to eat this hospital food since he's been here—"

"Let me help you." He shoots up. "I can drive you home. If you're hungry we can stop somewhere for lunch first."

"Oh — okay, I guess." He offers me a hand and I take it.

A minute later he's helping me into his Benz and then we're navigating through the streets toward Little Havana. It's only lunchtime, but the streets are bustling with walkers and Latin music. The atmosphere is lively and intoxicating. I have to suppress the smile on my face because I'm supposed to be grieving for the loss of my piece-of-shit father. But good riddance is all I can think. The truth is, seeing him in the hospital

40

this morning is the first time I've seen him in more than five years. And seeing him hooked up to all those machines and monitors is the most peaceful I've seen him ever.

"This is my favorite hole in the wall for lunch in all of Miami." He opens the passenger door for me. "I guess we missed official introductions: I'm Alex. What can I call you, Sugar?"

My smile tips at his sweet endearment as I take his hand to help me out of the car. "I like when you call me Sugar. Let's stick with that."

CHAPTER TEN

Genevieve

"Genevieve!" I groan when I hear Fawn calling my name. "Genevieve!" She calls out again and a few customers in The Wine Cellar turn and look. I force a smile on my lips as I turn to face Fawn. I was hoping to get all my errands finished up today without running into anyone I know. I can't win. I feel like I'm working off some shitty karma from a past life lately. "I've been calling you from across the aisles — didn't you hear me?" A trace of irritation flickers across Fawn's features before her measured smile returns.

"I didn't hear you, I'm sorry." I look down at my bottle of wine. "Trying to find the right bottle to go with dinner tonight. I've been so distracted lately."

"Oh, that's totally understandable. Don't even think about apologizing." Uncharacteristic warmth swims in her bright blue eyes. "Jerry's got me on the hunt for a specific pinot from Italy — one of his patients gave him a bottle of it last year. We just had it with lobster this past weekend and it was positively divine. He's hell-bent on getting more, even if we have to order it by the case from Italy!" She chuckles.

"He's been so stressed lately with his retirement and now this prescription shortage — he has clients calling the office all hours of the day and night asking for alternatives because they can't get their refills. It's been horrible — I'm thankful Jerry has access to samples or he'd be plum out of his blood pressure meds — I feel so bad for the seniors in our community. Jerry's doing what he can to work with the pharmaceutical reps but they're saying it's just a timing issue with production and delivery schedules. I don't understand any of it, I just hope it's over soon. Anyway, when in doubt pour a glass of wine, that's what I say!" Her eyes twinkle with mischief as she gestures to her basket where three bottles lay side by side. "I'm going to ask the manager if they're able to get that wine Jerry likes — I have a picture of the bottle on my phone. I'll send it to you — you and Alexandre should try it, I think you'd love it."

I nod, my head already splitting from her incessant rambling.

"Oh!" She begins again. "You'll be at Ken and Julianna's anniversary soirée tonight, right? It's been months since Jerry and I attended a black-tie, it took me forever to decide between a backless Prada dress and a vintage Halston I found at this sweet little shop on Ocean Avenue," she leans closer, "I still haven't decided which one to wear. We'll see what kind of mood I'm in at the eleventh hour, right?"

I nod, hardly able to form a sentence. My head feels so foggy and overwhelmed by this conversation. "Alexandre mentioned stopping in for a quick drink, I don't know if we can stay long though."

"Oh, no! You must! It's always so boring without you and Alexandre around at these things. What would you be doing at home, anyway? Watching tv or . . . I dunno, talking?" She giggles as if it's such a novel idea that I may want to spend alone time with my husband.

"Well, with Alexandre gone all week, our quality time is at a premium."

"I bet." Her eyes flick around the wine shop as if she's so done with this conversation, eager to move onto her next victim. "Well, I'd better get on with it. See you later tonight!"

Before I can even reply to her she's off in the direction of the checkout counter. I grind my teeth together at just the thought of enduring a night with the other wives. When we first moved to Kensington Bay, I spent so much time trying to fit in with these women, most of them trophy wives to older men, I never bothered to think about if I actually wanted to. Now, with everything else that's going on, all I want to do is dodge the countless questions and mindless gossip.

Once Fawn has purchased her wine and exits the store, I move to the checkout counter with my bottle of Bordeaux. I have half a mind to shoot Alexandre a quick text and tell him I'm not feeling well and not up to the party tonight, but he'd only worry about me more than he already does while he's away all week. I know he feels helpless being so far away and I know he's swamped with work, but I still struggle with feelings of neglect and abandonment.

As I slide behind the wheel of my Audi, I think for the first time since the children were born that maybe we rushed into having a family without giving ourselves enough time together. Alexandre and I were engaged within six months of our first meeting, twelve weeks later we were married on the beach at dawn, and a month later I found out I was pregnant. From the moment we first met our lives moved at hyperspeed. I never bothered to wonder if we were moving too fast because I'd never met anyone like him before — he fit like the lone puzzle piece missing in my heart. I clung to his closeness like sustenance, as if his absence would signal the dissolution of my health, stability, sanity.

Within minutes I'm pulling into the garage. As soon as the garage doors begin their slow descent, my heartbeat calms. I move into the house on slow footsteps, thinking a nap before Ken and Julianna's party tonight might be the only thing that's going to keep my headache at bay.

As if she's read my mind and is in direct opposition to my plan, Albertine comes racing down the stairs with a pair of child's scissors in one hand and construction paper in the other. "Maman! Maman! Look at my alligator!"

I drop to her level when she reaches me, radiant smile stretching my tired face. "It's beautiful, honey." In truth, I can't tell what it is she's made, but I can't say that. "We'll have to hang this on the fridge to show Daddy when he gets home." She nods with pride. "Also, what did I tell you about running with scissors?"

"That I shouldn't do it." She hangs her head. I instantly sense the defeat. I curse myself for turning her triumphant moment into another learning lesson — always worrying, always correcting, always criticizing. Is this what motherhood was meant to be? I don't think so, but I can't figure out any other way.

"Mommy and Daddy have a little party to go to tonight—"

"Can I come?" Her eyes shine with hope.

"No, this party is for grown-ups only." *Thank God.*

Albertine's frown slides a little deeper. "Can I watch a movie while you're gone?"

"Of course, baby. For a little while anyway." I pat her thin shoulders. "Mommy needs a little nap before Daddy and I leave tonight — how about you go upstairs and work on making me an entire alligator family and we'll tape them all on the fridge."

Her frown finally twitches into a smile. "Okay."

And with that she climbs the stairs, the little kid-sized scissors held carefully in one hand.

I set my things down on the kitchen counter, and then follow her up the stairs. When I pass her playroom I find her set up at her crafting table with tape and construction paper and piles of crayons. Albertine has always been good at entertaining herself, I'm thankful for that. I kick my heels off my feet when I enter my bedroom, collapsing on the king bed face first into the pillow. I let a soft groan fall off my lips as I think about the party tonight. My muscles feel weighted with lead, taut from the pain of carrying myself around all day pretending to be someone I'm not. Someone that fits into this life. My eyes fall closed briefly as I allow slow, measured breaths to take over my body. I think for a moment that a quick swim in the pool might wake me up, but then, I don't want to be woken. I just want to lie here and languish.

The next time my eyes flutter open I know it's late. Too late. I push out of bed to find the sun is close to setting. It must be seven at least — why didn't Alexandre wake me? We're supposed to be at Ken and Julianna's in an hour. I rub at my eyes to clear the sleep as I walk into the bathroom, then push my fingers through my long dark hair.

I freeze when I realize something isn't right.

My eyes snap to my reflection in the mirror. Tears burn my eyelids.

"Oh my God. What happened?" Chills course through me just as flames of heat crawl up my neck. I bite down on my lip, picking up a handheld mirror and turning to examine the back of my skull. My dark waves are messy and tangled from sleep, except at the top center of my head. There, a giant chunk of my hair is missing. As if it's been sheared off with a straight edge.

Scissors.

Albertine.

I run my fingertips along the fresh circle of stubble where my hair once was. How can I possibly cover this in time for the party? My salon is closed and anyway, I'd have to shave my head to match the length. I've been thinking about going shorter for a while, but a cute bob at most — not a military G.I. Jane style shave. The tears stream hot and fast down my cheeks. I want to drop to the floor and give up. Give up on being a mom. A wife. A woman I don't recognize anymore.

I search desperately for a lie I can tell the other wives at the party tonight. Something other than the fact that I'm a failure of a mother. Now, I'll wear my lack of maternal instincts like a brand. Is that what Albertine wanted? To mark me with her hatred? Announce my shortcomings as a mother to the world?

I sob, desperate for deliverance from this fate I've found myself in. I can't live inside of this life anymore.

And then a sense of fury climbs up my spine as I launch out of my bathroom and right down the hallway in the direction of Albertine's playroom. The room is empty but sitting in the center of the craft table are her tiny purple scissors and a freshly-sheared lock of my hair tied into knots and glued on top of an orange. I pick it up in my hands, examining it with shock as I find Albertine has drawn large red lips and blue eyes on the orange with a maker, and then sank at least a dozen push pins into the soft flesh of the fruit. It's like a little mommy voodoo doll.

Razor sharp blades claw at my throat.

Don't kill her. Don't kill her.

CHAPTER ELEVEN

Adeline

"This woman is so spoiled and narcissistic it's intolerable," I say to my reflection in the mirror as I wash my hands. The kids are napping and Gen is mimosa-drunk on the sofa watching old episodes of *Gilmore Girls*. She ran off to her stylist this morning for an emergency cut and style. She now sports an ultra-modern, side-part style that looks a little goth by Palm Beach standards. It's better than having a bald spot on the back of the head I suppose. Gen woke the house up in a fit this morning as she berated Albertine for cutting off a chunk of her hair while she napped yesterday afternoon. Alex and Gen canceled their plans last night and he spent the evening listening to her sob in bed about how ugly she is and how best to punish the little girl for her *violent act*, as Gen's been calling it.

I smile to myself, thinking how easy it'll be to push Gen to the edge. No wonder Alex left for Miami early — I can't stand to be around this woman either. I wonder if his absence today alters the household plan Gen keeps tacked to the corkboard in the pantry. I was supposed to make vegetarian lasagna for dinner tonight but now that the man of the house has left about as quickly as he arrived. I wonder if that menu still stands. I've only been here a few weeks and already I see Gen drinks her dinners and reheats the pre-made meals for the kids. I know she was once a working model; apparently, she still has the extremely limited diet of one too. For all the fancy Chanel she talks about, the clothes practically hang off of her frail form. As underfed as she looks though, the super-model diet isn't rare in Palm Beach. Most of the women look like Gen — underfed and over-medicated clutching their Louboutins and pearls.

In reality, it's no wonder Alex spends so little time with his wife. She's unbearable and not someone the Alex *I* used to know would have chosen for himself. Is it her that changed then? Or is it him? He's not the man I once knew, there's no doubt about that, but spending all of your free time with someone that's about as bland as mashed potatoes changes a person I guess. I can't help but wonder what he gets up to in a flashy city like Miami all week. I imagine dinner and drinks with clients at lively hot spots downtown or in Little Havana. Fat cigars and Cuban dancers salsa in my mind's eye.

Maybe he's even got a girlfriend in Miami. Or a *few* of them.

"Adeline!" Gen calls from the sofa.

I wipe my hands on the towel and then head back to the living room. Gen is sprawled on the couch, her cream linen pants are wrinkled and spotted with mimosa stains. She looks like a drunk, plain and simple, but I do my best not to judge.

"What do you need, Ms.?" I say when I'm within earshot.

"The baby — he won't stop crying. Can you check on him? Maybe he needs a bottle or a bath?" Her words are slurred. I bet she doesn't even know what time of day it is.

"I'll handle it, Ms."

I think how truly vulnerable she is in this moment. If she only knew the truth about me. If only she knew how very well I know her husband. And how I plan to get to know him again. She is a sitting duck; a fat little pig with her belly turned

49

up, lounging in the sun while I sit like a lion in wait, ready to pounce when she least expects it.

Genevieve has gone soft. Life has spoiled her. Because she was born with a certain arrangement of features that deem her attractive to most people, she's been given everything in life and existed in a bubble of bottomless champagne and Chanel.

I choke down the ball of bitterness that sits in my throat. I have arrived, I remind myself. I've made it to my final destination: right here — *with him*. Will he recognize me? I doubt it. And by the time he does it will be too late. Far, far too late.

I enter the baby's nursery. Gen must be delusional because I haven't heard the baby cry once this afternoon — but he is awake. He's sitting on his bottom in the crib, babbling to himself in his own language while he plays with a stuffed teddy. "Hey, little guy."

Laurent's eyes light up when he sees me. His round cheeks are still red with sleep. I lift him out of the crib and bring him to the changing table but he's not having any of it. He's squirming and wiggling and the longer I hold him the angrier he gets. I try to hum and rock him on my hip to soothe him but all he wants is away from me. It's like this kid has a sixth sense for danger. He's certainly already more astute than his mother. "Laurent — Laurent—" I try to hush him — "You stink, buddy. We just need to change this diaper and then you can run free."

I drop to my knees and lay him on the plush wool rug. He wriggles and whines but I manage to get the diaper off of him. As soon as I do he twists like an acrobat and crawls away from me. He's already headed out of the nursery door. This kid is on a mission to get as far the hell away from me as he can and I can't say I blame him. I'm ready to throttle this kid. "Ugh — dammit. Laurent!"

He turns, rests on his little bottom a moment and then smiles back at me with a wide toothy grin.

"Come on, buddy — wanna take a bath?" I'm cooing softly, doing my best not to startle him like the little wild animal that he is. Just as I'm within distance, he scoots off again. But he's not so quick this time and I catch him by just an ankle. He tries to kick me off and then starts wailing when he realizes he's been caught. "You're lucky I have more patience than my mom—" I scoop him in my arms as an errant memory of my mother yelling at me as I look up at her from a bubble bath flashes in my mind. I don't know what age I am in the memory, but I would say not more than three or four — only a little younger than the age Albertine is now. I push the emotions down that have bubbled up with this particular memory; I buried most of my family skeletons under layers of cynicism and dark humor, but being in the Moreau-DuPont home has been triggering to say the least.

When Laurent and I reach the bathroom, I wrangle him out of the rest of his clothes and then flip the water on for the bath. Laurent is instantly interested and trying to pull himself up on the edge of the bath. He isn't walking quite yet, but he's ready. I add a few pumps of bubble bath to the water and then test to make sure it's not too hot or cold before lifting the little guy into the tub. His smile widens and I see the tiniest pearly white tooth just starting to pop through his gums. Gen is missing so much wallowing on that Italian leather sofa she's so attached to.

At that moment, a scream pierces the house.

"Albertine?!" I call out but it's hard to hear anything over the rushing bath water. I flip the water faucet off and then encourage Laurent to sit on his bottom. "Albertine?!"

"Help!" The little girl calls back. I groan, wishing her mother would shake out of her stupor and do something about the screaming five-year-old.

"Coming!" I call back to Albertine. I drop a few rubber duckies in the soapy water and Laurent starts splashing and playing with them. "I'll be right back. Don't move, okay?"

Laurent ignores me and splashes away. I dart from the bathroom and down the long hallway. It takes me longer than it should because despite the fact that the nursery and Albertine's room are in the same wing of the house, they're about a mile apart with the theater room and an upstairs playroom that's basically the size of the shack I grew up in in the space between. There's also an actual bowling alley in the playroom too, but Gen didn't show me that on the house tour. I discovered that on my own when Albertine and I played hide-and-seek yesterday and she hid behind the bowling pins. It took me an hour to find her and by the time I did I was so irritated I called the game and put the little girl down for a nap. I don't even know if she takes naps anymore, but as long as I'm here she will be.

"Albertine?" I call as I approach the doorway of her room. She's been playing quietly with dolls and stuffed animals all afternoon, perhaps I've neglected her a bit the last few hours, but in all fairness, I've been dealing with her mother tanked off mimosas on the couch.

"Help, please!" Albertine's voice is tiny now. As I enter the room I know instantly something is wrong.

"Albertine? Where are you?"

"Here," comes her little voice.

"Where?"

"In the closet. I'm stuck." I can hear the tears in her words.

I open the accordion doors of her closet and push through piles of blankets and patent leather shoes. "I don't see you."

"Not *that* closet, silly."

"What other closet?" Agitation rises in my voice.

"This one!" She calls from what still sounds like far away. "Behind my desk."

"Behind the desk. Behind the desk . . ." My eyes land on the white desk in the corner. It's stacked with volumes of nursery rhymes and a reading light, and beneath it is a small square trapdoor that looks just barely bigger than a doggy door.

"Albertine?" I bend and whisper.

"The door is locked. I'm stuck!"

"Oh, sweet Jesus." I try the handle and she's right. I don't think it's locked because the knob turns easily, but it does seem to be jammed. "Just a minute, honey." She doesn't reply but I hear her small whimpers. "It's okay, I'm right here."

She sobs and sniffs. My heart cracks. I rattle the door-knob gently and then with more strength. "Is there a key to this door, Albertine?"

"No," comes a choked sob.

"Is there something blocking the door on your side?" My breaths are becoming shallow. Fuck. I wish Genevieve were here. I suddenly realize exactly what she's been managing alone with two kids all week long. Then I realize Albertine still hasn't answered me. "Albertine, honey?"

Still no answer. I rattle the door harder. Nothing budges. How did the little miscreant get in there in the first place if it's this hard to open the door? I wedge my sneaker against the wall beside the door jamb and then yank with all my might. The door swings open and I fall back and hit my head against the leg of the desk. "Shit!"

"That's a bad word! I'm telling Daddy!" Albertine is crouching over me with an angry face. I scrunch my eyes closed and take a deep breath and count to five before I open my eyes again. "Albertine — were you holding the door closed?"

"Nope!" She sticks her tongue out at me, pinches my arm and then leaps out from under the desk and I notice then that the inside of the crawl space is lined with a menagerie of stuffed animals and dolls. "It was Puppy!" She snuggles the little stuffed dog under her chin, her bright blue eyes sparkling as she stands at the doorway.

"You hurt me, Albertine." I hold a palm over my tender flesh, certain she'll have left me with a bruise by morning. I puff out an exhausted breath and then crawl off the floor. "Were you really stuck?" She only shrugs. "It's not very nice to lie, ya know. Don't your parents teach you manners?" I say that last part under my breath. "Your brother's in the bath — I don't have time for these little games, Albertine. Why don't you go downstairs and jump on the couch for a while." A dark grin lifts my lips as I think about Gen waking up, hungover with a kid bouncing on her fine Italian leather.

Albertine isn't listening though. She's already running down the hallway at full speed. A flash of a horrible accident blinks in my vision as I imagine her tripping on her long pink polka dot dress and taking a tumble. It's not that I wish a tragic accident on this kid, but I do wish she'd make my life a little easier right now by behaving herself. "Hey, Albertine?" I call after her. "Do you have an iPad you could play games on for a while your brother finishes his bath?"

"No electronics until after dinner, that's the rule!" She shrieks and hangs a sharp right into the bathroom. "Uh oh! I'm gonna tell on you!"

My heart falls. What's she talking about? I speed up my steps and follow her into the bathroom. I halt as I watch Albertine slap at her brother's belly and giggle, "Why are his lips blue?"

"Oh no — Laurent?" I rush to the side of the bathtub to find the little boy still as stone and his skin a sickly shade of gray. And Albertine is right — his lips are dark blue. I scoop him from the water and instantly notice that it's freezing. This kid is practically in shock. "Oh fuck, oh fuck, oh fuck."

"That's a bad word!" Albertine sings and dances around the bathroom, her pretty pink dress swirling around her bare feet.

"Albertine — shut up and go get me blankets from your bed. Your brother is freezing to death." I wrap him in a heated towel from the warming bin and rub up and down his little body to generate friction. "Please, just listen to me, Albertine. Go get me some blankets so we can warm your brother up."

"He's dead! He's dead!" She twirls and dances as my blood runs cold.

"No — Albertine — stop. Please stop saying that." Hot tears wet my cheeks as I try to think of any way to generate more heat for this little boy. I start humming a lullaby to him because if I don't I think I'll drown in a pool of my own tears. I carry him to a bright beam of sunshine that cuts through the window and I sway back and forth, rubbing all of his limbs, and then his tiny fingers, and then pressing my own face to his chilled cheeks.

"He's dead! He's dead!" Albertine sings.

"Shut up!" I hiss at the little brat. This seems to get her attention. She stops, narrows her eyes in a resentful glare and then lifts one eyebrow at me. The little beast is intimidating, I'll give her that. She's already a mini- Stepford wife in training — Gen may not feel like one of those haughty spoiled women, but her daughter already is.

Laurent wiggles in my arms then, his eyes drowsy as he snuggles against my neck and begins sucking his thumb.

"Oh God, thank you," I breathe in prayer. "See?" I bend to Albertine's height so she can see into her brother's warm brown eyes. "He's fine. Everything is fine. It was just a close call, that's all." Her eyes shift from mine to her brother's and back again. As if she doesn't believe me. "He's going to be just fine."

"His lips are blue," she states. Her face is expressionless and it causes a chill to run through my blood.

"No — not anymore. See?" I turn my body to show her.

She frowns then runs out of the bathroom singing, "He's dead! He's dead! *Le petit prince* is dead in his bed!"

I groan, realizing finally that she's been singing some stupid little nursery rhyme this entire time.

"Ugh, Albertine." I bite my tongue to prevent the string of swears falling from my lips.

"I'm telling Daddy you swore!" Her giggle is wicked.

"You wouldn't." I narrow my eyes at her. "I won't let you have ice cream after dinner if you tell."

"We never have ice cream after dinner." She crosses her arms and stares back at me.

"Perfect — how about I let you have a big bowl of ice cream after dinner tonight if you promise not to tell anyone what I said?"

She doesn't answer but her lips twist into a cunning smirk. "With hot fudge?"

"Fine." I spit.

"And marshmallows?"

She's negotiating. I'm negotiating with a five-year-old. "Marshmallows are disgusting."

"I love them. They're my favorite." She's cool, calm, and calculated and it unnerves me to the core.

"Fine. Marshmallows *and* fudge."

Her grin turns big and toothy before she dances off down the stairs ahead of me. "He's dead! He's dead!" She sings. "Can I go in the pool now?"

I groan. Gen is catatonic the last I checked. If Albertine gets in the pool now, it'll be only me watching her. I blink away exhaustion as I realize I'm not getting paid nearly enough to pretend to be Gen while she fucks off in a champagne coma.

The lives of the rich and famous are far less glamorous than they'd have you believe. In fact, Genevieve Moreau-DuPont is just as trashy as the trailer park moms I grew up with, she just wears pearls when she slurs orders at her kids.

A realization strikes me then. There's nothing that separates Gen and I after all; she is a hot mess express and I am the snake in the grass ready to slide all that she holds dear out from under her when the time is right.

CHAPTER TWELVE

Genevieve

"I've already spoken to the pharmacist — there's nothing they can do—"

"Maybe there's a place in Miami that can fill it." Alexandre interrupts me. He's distracted. I can tell. We always spend a few minutes when he gets to work in the morning checking in on the phone and again at night before bed. We've been doing this since he started working in Miami all week — but lately, lately I can't deny that he's been different. Lately, my husband feels like a stranger in my life. We go through the routine, but something is missing.

"There's a national shortage—"

"Then we wait it out — it'll be fine. Keep me posted. Listen, I have to jump into a meeting this morning with the partners, chat later tonight, okay?" His tone is clipped. He speaks to me like I'm a child and it makes my skin crawl.

"Okay," I say, feeling chastised.

"Talk to you later," he utters and then I swear I hear a soft, feminine chuckle. Instantly my veins heat as if fire ants crawl under my skin.

Before I can reply he's already hung up.

"Thanks," I say into the void before dropping my phone on the kitchen counter. "Thanks a lot."

"Trouble in paradise, Ms.?" Adeline appears out of the ether.

"Oh!" I hold a hand over my hammering heart. "You scared me."

"I'm sorry." Adeline says simply. She's a woman of few words — I like that she doesn't fill the space with needless noise. But it also makes me even more curious about what's going on in her head.

"And no — no trouble. I was just wishing Alexandre a good morning." I wipe down the already clean counter with a towel. "How are the children? Is Albertine ready for school?"

"She is." She turns to the fridge and pulls orange juice from the shelf. She rummages around in a cupboard before pouring two glasses then turning to face me. She slides one of them across the counter with a genuine smile. "Orange juice, Ms.?"

"I told you," I grunt, "call me Gen when we're alone."

"Sure, I'm sorry — *Gen*."

"I think I'll take Albertine to school this morning and stop at the coffee shop after — please make sure Laurent is bathed and dressed for the day when I get home. We have a lunch playdate with some of the other wives at noon."

Adeline nods, then busies herself with putting away the clean dishes from the dishwasher.

"Did you see my husband at all this weekend?" I ask, curiosity getting the better of me.

"No."

I nod. "I didn't think so. He doesn't think we need help — he's uncomfortable with a stranger in the house." She doesn't respond so I continue. "You're hardly a stranger though — I mean, you're an au pair by trade. He's just so distrustful of people — I know he's just being cautious but I am a pretty good judge of character. I mean, I picked him, right?"

"I'm ready for school!" Albertine skips into the room in mismatched everything.

"Honey — please — you know you need to wear your uniform." I tuck a piece of hair behind Albertine's ear with a frown.

"I don't want to." Albertine pouts then wraps a piece of my hair in her little hand and yanks. A look of glee fills her face as my eyes water with the pain.

"Stop it!" I pry open her grip and free myself. I smash my lips together because if I don't I'll call this devil child every swear word in the book. Instead, I back away and say with a measured breath, "Adeline, will you please help her?" I turn on my heel, annoyance radiating through me. "We're going to be late, Albertine, come on. Hurry up." I shoot Adeline a withering glance.

A forced smile crosses her face, but not before I catch the flicker of an emotion I can't quite place. Like she's just tasted the most bitter lemon, the sharp acid burning her tongue and contorting her features with disdain. Impatience leaks out of my tone when I say my next words, "What am I paying you for if you can't keep the children on schedule? Next time, please have Albertine ready at eight fifteen sharp or we'll need to discuss alternative arrangements."

Adeline's face falls, her eyes go to the floor before she scoots Albertine down the hallway with her. There. That will teach them both to cross me.

CHAPTER THIRTEEN

Adeline

I hope the sleeping pills Gen didn't know she'd just taken make her a sound sleeper. I have a lot of patience, but I can't take over this woman's life *and* deal with her high-strung outbursts and derogatory orders on top of it. It's not like I was planning to drug her upon waking up this morning, but if that's what it takes to get some peace in this house, I'm not above it.

Plus, it gives me time to find out what's really going on behind these whitewashed walls.

"Hm . . . What do we have here?" I lift an empty bottle of pills from the vanity. Genevieve Moreau-DuPont is printed on the label. The medication is expired and I'm not quite sure what it's for, I can't even pronounce the name, but if I had to guess I would imagine it's some designer mommy drug made to treat low-level anxiety that afflicts every other housewife in this gated commune.

I crack a smile as I think about the other wives — *the mommy cult* — as I've taken to thinking of them. Gen brings them up often — and meeting that mommy zombie at the market was interesting to say the least. I get the same feeling Gen does when she's with them — like just below the superficial pleasantries lies a barrage of criticisms and judgments just waiting to fight their way out. Maybe I've watched too many *Real Housewives of Wherever* episodes, but too much Botox and lip filler triggers me at this stage.

I set the empty pill bottle back in its place and then close the mirror vanity and move into Gen and Alex's room. I've never been in here because Gen's never left me in the house alone before. A massive king bed sits in the middle of their bedroom facing an entire wall of windows that overlook the pool area. This must be where Gen was arguing with her husband the other day — and the entire time they had a perfect view of Albertine and I at the pool. A shiver courses through me as I realize from this vantage point, the masters of the house have a view of their entire estate. Gen can lounge mimosa-drunk all day from her bed and watch me tend her kids like she's viewing animals at the zoo through safety glass. Was that her intention? To find someone else to raise her kids so she can . . . what? Languish in self-pity all day?

It's not clear to me what Gen wants beyond barking orders at the help.

I slide open the top drawer of her bureau. A dozen bras in various shades are tucked neatly in the drawer. I slide the next open and find perfectly folded beige and black panties as far as the eye can see. I dig through a few of them looking for any personal items tucked in the silky folds. Just when I think Gen is as boring as I imagined, I find an envelope. It's open, with pages of what looks like handwritten letters inside. Slipping the folded pages out, a zap of excitement courses through me when I realize what I've found.

They're love letters. All to Gen from Alex, and they're all dated in the years before the kids were born. I skim the text for anything interesting but find nothing more than the standard *I love you to the ends of the earth* bullshit lovers say to each other in the new stages of a relationship. Before diapers and dishes and pre-made dinners I imagine there were date nights and engraved jewelry and long weekends in the Bahamas.

I slip the love letters back where they belong and close the drawer.

I wonder what he sees in her. Gen is generic — as dull as canned peas as far as I can tell. She's not aware enough to recognize it, but the things she dislikes about the other wives are the very things she dislikes in herself. Game recognize game. I see it, but poor Gen is too wrapped up in herself to see who it really is she's judging. I make no claim to knowing anything more than the next person — my public-school education has gotten me this far, which really isn't much to write home about, but I have been around successful women long enough to know that their egos are often the most wounded with just a sideways glance. Women who live in gated communes like this one sense their vulnerability and lash out like tigers in a cage at any perceived threat. Gen knows that she's replaceable — that's why she calls me the help — to remind me of my place while fluffing her own ego in the process.

I move to the other bureau of drawers and slide the top open. Inside are Alex's neatly folded underthings, along with a small tray of gleaming cufflinks and a Rolex. A charge of emotion overwhelms me at the sight of it. I blink away errant tears and lift it in my hands, turning it over and caressing the shiny watch-face as memories of *before* swallow me. Candlelit dinners and moonlit walks and cozy Sunday mornings by the fireplace. I wonder if he's blocked it all out in favor of this life — the one he's chosen *without* me.

Agitation swells like a tidal wave as I think of all that he has gained and all I have lost.

While he attains the life he's always dreamed of — the status and success and freedom — I sit here tending to his family. The irony of it makes my heart beat triple speed. I imagine the terror that would fill him if he knew the truth of what his wife has done — who exactly she's hired to take care of his most precious cargo.

"Well, if they were so precious you wouldn't leave them to the wolves, would you?" I smirk, sliding the drawer closed. I can't help but dream about what it would be like to show him what fun is again. It's already clear to me that where his wife is neurotic, I am playful. Where she is high strung when he comes home from a week at work, I could help him unwind and relax like we used to — bubble baths and slow Sunday afternoons spent in the kitchen drinking wine and trying new recipes. I can't help but imagine what a date would look like for us now, after all this time. Is he playful like he once was? Or have kids and a marriage stolen that from him too? I certainly can't imagine the Gen I see before me now — cold, distracted, and detached — is the Gen who said *I do* on their wedding day. *Or is she?*

Maybe after *us* he wanted someone like *her* — someone as opposite from me as possible.

Resentment builds as I think of what could have been and all that was lost between us. But this is my chance. My chance to have it all. There are just a few bumps in the road that I have to overcome first. Three very real obstacles that won't be so easy to erase, but with time, all things are possible.

"Adeline?" Gen's thready voice calls through the house. My eyes dart around the room one last time to make sure I'm not leaving behind any evidence of my presence.

"Coming, Ms.!" With a satisfied smile, I walk out of Gen and Alex's bedroom on easy strides.

I haven't been in the Moreau-DuPont house long and already I know their inner workings — the way he calls her each morning before he begins work and again before bed. How they've been sleeping in separate bedrooms since Albertine was born. What Gen spends all of her free time doing — sipping cocktails and worrying about the nonsense of rich and famous people. And who she likes to avoid: the mommy cult that walks around Palm Beach like they own it. Now, I only have to figure out their why; why they keep up the ruse of happiness when they're both so obviously drowning.

Why they speak twice a day all week long and hardly at all when he's home on the weekends. Why hibernating in the man cave has become the alternative to family time.

And once I know the why, it will make the when so much easier. I am the last missing piece of this puzzle — the storm they never saw coming. By the time I'm finished, the lives of Genevieve and Alexandre Moreau-DuPont will be forever altered. Their home will never be the same.

"Adeline?!" Gen's shriek echoes up the stairwell.

"Coming, Ms.!" I yell a little louder before plastering a fake smile on my face.

Taking out Gen will be the highlight of my time here. One slow, measured step at a time I will dismantle her sanity until she can't tell right from wrong, black from white, love from hate, trust from evil.

I am a force to be reckoned with, but for now, Gen must believe I'm as gentle as a newborn bird, fearful of everything and eager to please. And just when she thinks she has a hold of me — it will be her I'm kicking out of the nest.

Because now that I'm here, I don't plan on leaving.

CHAPTER FOURTEEN

Genevieve

"Albertine had a presentation at school today — I wasn't able to be there though. I was doing a deep clean of the freezer and completely lost track of time." The lie is smooth on my lips. Really, it was Adeline cleaning the freezer, but what's a little white lie for the sake of keeping the peace?

"That sounds nice." Alexandre says. He's clearly distracted but it's not unusual for him. I expect him to have his head in the game all week long while he's in Miami, it's just when he's home and still distracted that it starts to get to me. "Tell Albertine I'm so proud of her and if I could have been there I would."

"Sure," I say brightly. I wish he would come home during the week sometimes for special occasions such as this, but then, there will be more. Albertine is young and will hardly remember these moments, it's me that will have to live with them.

"Give our girl a goodnight kiss for me." Alexandre interrupts my thoughts.

"I will. We miss you," I say as an afterthought.

He hums in agreement. "Have a good night."

"I love you," I say but instead of the typical *I love you* that usually comes as a reply, I hear the sound of a woman's laugh in the background. My heart clenches in my chest. My husband has a private office and often works late at night with the partners — but all of the partners at his firm are men.

"Hey—" I begin to ask but realize the line is already dead. Alexandre hung up without saying I love you. He *always* says I love you.

I set my phone down on the counter and then wipe down the polished granite with a hand towel.

"Ms.? I just wanted to tell you that Laurent went down peacefully and Albertine has asked if she can play in the pool before bed." Adeline clamps down on her bottom lip. "Are you okay, Ms.?"

"Yes — Adeline — I'm fine. As fine as I can be, I guess." The dull pounding in my head has begun again, the slow throbbing sound of it washing over me in waves. I put my hands to my face just to feel if it's still there.

Adeline's eyes flash down to her hands and then she frowns. "Did you get bad news from Miami?"

"Hm?"

"Your husband, Ms. — did you get bad news from your husband? You look upset."

"Oh — I guess there's no point in hiding it, huh?" I smile. "I've always had trouble hiding my thoughts and feelings — I guess that makes me a terrible liar. I even told Alexandre that I cleaned the freezer and that's why I missed Albertine's Earth Day presentation — does that make me a bad mom? I just couldn't stand the thought of sitting through a day at school with all the other wives." A shiver courses through me. "You think I'm awful, don't you?"

"I don't. Not at all." Adeline smiles sweetly, then places a warm hand on top of mine. "We're all just doing our best — even your husband. It must be so hard for him to be away from his family all week."

"Is it though?" I say out loud before I can stop myself. "Sometimes I wonder." Adeline doesn't reply so I continue. "Maybe it's just the break he's looking for — would you think I'm terrible if I said most weeks I'm jealous that he gets to leave? Sometimes I wonder what it would have been like if I kept my career and his took a back seat. I could have — it was an option. I made enough money for us to live on for a lifetime — our children too because I invested it in the market and the dividends pay even bigger now than they did. We had so many options, so why does it feel like mine are gone?" I turn and catch a glimpse of myself in a wall mirror that hangs next to the pantry door. My shoulder-length hair is wrangled in a braided side bun with a severe side-part meant to disguise the missing chunk from Albertine's scissors. "Every day I wake up and I don't recognize myself. Now I'm just old and have crow's feet and nobody wants to pay to see a middle-aged woman in a bathing suit." I press my lips together and then purse them into a perfect pout — the pout that I was known for — the pout that walked runways in Paris and Milan and sold magazine covers around the world. Now my lips are wrinkled and thin. "Maybe it's time I got a little lip filler." I spin, catching sight of Adeline watching me. "What do you think? Just enough to give me my pout back."

"I don't think you need it — you're beautiful."

"Oh, well I know compared to most women I still stand out, but that's not good enough. I want to be the kind of beautiful my husband married. I want to be . . . the girl I was before all of this." I gesture into the air to indicate all of it — this life, this family, the chains that are weighing me down.

"I knew motherhood would take everything out of me, but at this point it's taking more than I have to give. Albertine's birth was a breeze — my water broke at home and she was crying her way into this world two hours later. I was foolish enough to think that everything about her would be a breeze, like we were meant to be together, but I was so wrong. The nightmare began the day we brought her home. Breastfeeding was awful — my milk never came in and Albertine had the most terrible time latching — it's like something in her knew my body was poison. It felt like rejection on day one, and then we could never find a formula that didn't make her tummy upset. The all-night crying fits broke me.

"So when I found out I was pregnant with Laurent, I nearly lost my mind. Every single moment of the pregnancy was horrible. First it started with the heartburn, and then came the morning sickness that never ended . . . I was exhausted constantly and trying to keep up with Albertine and all I could think was what a giant mistake I'd made. Some women are made for motherhood and I am not one of them. At the beginning of my second trimester I was diagnosed with high blood pressure and by the end of it I was on bed-rest and begging them to take him out early. I didn't care if he'd have to live on a ventilator for a few weeks, he would have survived just fine — but I wasn't sure that I would if he wasn't evicted soon. Pregnancy almost killed me, I should have known that his birth would be even worse. I started bleeding at home — the ambulance came and I was rushed to the birthing center where I had an emergency c-section. It was so traumatic for all of us. Albertine thought I was dying." I push the wetness that's accumulated in my eyes. "The great revelation about motherhood never came for me. Instead, if I'm lucky, there are these little daily miracles, small, sweet moments like matches struck in the dark to light the way. But the more time goes on, the less glimmers of light there are. Alexandre didn't seem phased by all the trauma it took to bring Laurent into this world though and he was the sweetest little baby. There's a certain purity to a being that doesn't speak yet. Albertine rebelled from the time she had words to, but not my boy. Never my boy. He was a spoonful of sugar every day, he even slept better than Albertine ever did." I sigh, wearing the guilt and shame of my failed connection to motherhood like a cloak. "Do you want children, Adeline?" I turn to her. She's watching me carefully, as if she doesn't know how to answer this question.

"No, I don't think that's in the cards for me." Comes her reply.

"I like that you know that — I like that you're not chasing someone else's dream for your life. When I met Alexandre everything just seemed to fall into place, we moved so fast, like we'd just been waiting to find each other. He proposed to me six months after we met, we were married three months later, and I came back from our honeymoon with a positive pregnancy test. We were overjoyed — but we had no idea what we were in for. No one does, I guess, but we had so little time together before we started a family something . . . just . . . *broke*. How could I have known the very foundations of our relationship would never be the same after we had children? The very thing I relied on disintegrated one sleepless night at a time. Nothing is the same — I've started thinking about our life together as either *before* children or *after* — and then with him gone all week . . . well, how are we supposed to be *us?* We're apart all the damn time — couples are supposed to grow together but all we're doing is growing apart all week long."

"You should talk to him. I'm sure he's feeling the same way you are."

I shake my head, seeds of doubt already planted beneath my skin like bad weeds. "No — I know when something is off with my husband. I can feel it in my bones — this man has a secret."

CHAPTER FIFTEEN

Adeline

I've been lingering on Gen's words all afternoon.

This man has a secret.

I think she's right. Something is up with him; the way he so artfully avoids his family is suspicious. If I were Gen I'd be down in Miami right now trying to figure out exactly what that man's secret is. But, because Gen has a spine as strong as spaghetti, I've decided to do her job for her.

I spent most of the afternoon cleaning the upstairs while Gen lounged by the pool, sipping champagne she doesn't know is dosed with a sedative. And while she sunbathed, I snooped. First in their bedroom in search of anything that might indicate what Alex spends his time doing in Miami all week. I found restaurant receipts, work statements, and blueprints for various buildings around Miami in a file cabinet hidden away in their walk-in closet. Nothing that indicates anything unusual. In fact, based on my findings, Alex is as boring as his wife.

Until I find myself in his office. This is where he spends all of his time when he's in Palm Beach; if this man has secrets worth finding, this is where they'll be. I'm sure of it. First, I was able to find an extra key card and the lease agreement for his one-bedroom apartment. The place must be luxury because the rent runs over $4,000 a month for just a one-bedroom. Obviously, this isn't a place he brings the kids. He's got his own bona fide bachelor pad right downtown and according to the lease, it's all paid for up front by his firm.

I keep digging and find his work contract. Alex is pulling in a cool quarter million a year on salary plus profit-sharing with the firm. This puts him in an upper income bracket that I can't even begin to fathom — plus with Gen's modeling money . . . the Moreau-DuPonts are a power couple.

So why don't they act like it? In fact, why does it seem like their marriage is a barely cobbled together union of convenience?

An idea percolates to life about just how I could prove that this man is more than he lets on. I move back to the closet in search of the lease agreement. When I find it, I snap a photo on my phone and then pocket the spare key card before leaving his office. I move into his man cave where I find a massive expanse of space filled with large pieces of workout equipment, bookshelves, and a flat-screen tv mounted on the wall. It occurs to me what a difference my perception was the first time I walked up to this elegant estate compared to now. In just a few short weeks all of my illusions of grandeur have dissipated and been replaced with liquor-soaked sadness and despair.

I make my way up the stairs and just as I reach the landing in the main hall I hear Gen's phone chirp with a new text message. I listen for her soft footsteps but nothing comes. She's probably passed out who knows where. The phone chirps again and I follow the sound into the kitchen. Her phone sits on the counter, the notification indicates a new message from Alex.

My mission crystallizes then.

I pick up the phone in the hopes that Gen doesn't have a passcode. She doesn't and it unlocks quickly.

I'm in.

I navigate to her text message inbox and find the most recent from Alex.

Left the file for the Flamingo Bay condos on my nightstand — I need it for a meeting tomorrow morning. Would love if you could deliver it tonight — we could go for dinner after.

A knowing grin lifts my lips. This is my chance. Gen is wasted — too drunk to drive. I'll step in and save the day.

My reply is quick: *I'll make sure you have it by morning :)*

Alex's text comes moments later. *Perfect. I'll make a reservation for 8.*

I send a kiss emoji in reply and then swipe right on the conversation. It vanishes instantly. And just like that, I have dinner plans.

I spend the next hour feeding the kids and then getting ready — it's nearly five as is. It will take me at least an hour to get downtown to Alex's apartment. I've already nicked a short black dress with a deep v cutting down my torso from Gen's walk-in. The dress is open nearly to my belly button and not the kind of style I would ever pick for myself, but I can see why Gen would. She yearns for attention and validation at her core and I'm sure with the help of this little black dress she received it in spades.

By the time the sun is kissing the horizon, I have a fully-winged cat-eye in the blackest eyeliner I have and a cherry red lipstick staining my lips. I am unrecognizable. This sexy, fussy look doesn't suit me at all, but it's fun to play pretend for a while. I throw on a long black coat, stop for Alex's files on his nightstand, and then check on the baby. He's been playing in his playpen all afternoon, content to flip through books and play flashy little kids' games on my phone while I get ready. I know it's unlikely that Gen will wake up — even if this kid starts screaming she'll probably sleep through it. I change his diaper quickly and leave him with a warm bottle just in case Gen is lights out for the night.

Albertine has been camped in front of the television in the playroom for the last hour — she's already eaten one of the pre-made meals Gen had in the freezer so when I stop to see her I bring a bowl of ice cream topped with fudge and marshmallows, just how she likes it. Her smile brightens when she sees me. I tell her I'll be back in a little bit and to be a good girl while I'm gone. She nods happily and then crushes me in a tight hug before I go. Her display of affection is unusual — at five she already has a pretty large chip on her shoulder, but every kid needs hugs and I guess a hug from a stranger is better than a hug from an alcoholic mother.

My first impression of the little girl was a harsh one. Her cold attitude was off-putting, but now I understand this apple didn't fall far from the tree. In fact, maybe Albertine and I have more in common than I imagined. We both were cursed with self-involved mothers preoccupied with their own personal drama. Love is learned and without a nurturing parent to blaze the path, what remains is a void where connection and comfort belong. At five, this little girl has constructed a coat of armor to protect her fragile soul from the world. While her mother wears a costume of designer dresses and rouged lips, Albertine has already masked herself with anger and resentment.

Albertine snuggles into her pillow as a sleepy smile tilts her lips. I find myself growing more drawn to the little girl with each passing day. I usually make a habit of not getting attached. I've never found it useful, if anything vulnerability is a weakness that taints my decision-making and plants seeds of false hope.

I think of Laurent's chubby little fingers and sweet smile and wonder if he's destined for the same fate as poor Albertine — searching for scraps of her mother's love. I suddenly feel like maybe my purpose here has been made more clear — this isn't just about Alex and Gen anymore, this runs deeper. If showing these kids the love they've been starved for all week will help me attain my goals, I'm here for it.

I flip off the lights, sighing as I leave Albertine's bedroom with the realization that I've probably bitten off more than I can chew with this family, but there's no rewinding time now. I'm knee-deep in shit and the only way out is through, as my dad liked to say.

Another minute later and I'm sliding behind the wheel of Gen's Audi and backing out of the garage. I'm free. I have the chance to step into another woman's heels for a night and the feeling sends tendrils of exhilaration through me. I drive in a haze as I think of all the ways Alex and I can reconnect — will he recognize me now? Even when I was younger this isn't an outfit I would pick for myself but it's fun to dress up — I don't remember when the last time was that I had a reason to wear red lipstick. My excitement builds with each passing mile marker. I've made the trip to Miami a million times over the years — it was the first place my friends and I went when we wanted a night out on the town, but this night feels so different. Tonight is a reunion.

Luckily, my trip into Miami goes by quickly and less than an hour after I left Palm Beach, I'm parallel parking the Audi in front of Alex's apartment building downtown. The building is a massive, modern marvel. Some of the glass is frosted a soft seafoam shade and as the eye crawls up, the reflection of the bay and the ever-blue Florida skies makes for a striking halo of cyan hues depending on which angle the sunlight hits. A contemporary sculpture in the same frosted seafoam glass anchors the entrance into the building. Lush palms are scattered around the property and bougainvillea trellises overlooking koi ponds offer small nooks to pause and linger awhile. The building is luxury — no wonder Alex has an apartment here. In fact, the thought occurs to me that maybe this building is one of Alex's designs. If this is his work, he's talented, there's no doubt about it.

I smooth the hem of my dress as I climb out of the Audi, then walk on long strides up the sidewalk to the entrance of the building. I swipe my key card at the double glass doors and they slide open soundlessly. I suck in a nervous breath and then hold my head high and walk through the lobby as if

I own the place. I'm surprised to find there is no bellman or concierge in the lobby, but it's better for me that there isn't. I pass the key card against the elevator and the doors open. I step in, then punch the button to take me to the fourteenth floor, which, based on the lease in Alex's office, is where his apartment is. I'm just checking the time on my watch when the doors slide open again and a man in fine brown leather shoes steps in with me. My eyes crawl up his lean form as my heart clatters in my ears.

It's him.

It's been so long since I've been with him like this and now that I'm here the only thing I want to do is run the other way.

His eyes flick up and down my body before a slow grin lifts his lips. I gulp down my anxiety, clutching his file to my chest as my heart hammers. "Hi."

His gaze is almost too intense, like looking directly at the sun. "Is that my file?"

I nod as my eyes land on his simmering hazel irises. "I tried to get here as fast as I could — you probably didn't expect—"

"It's perfect. Thank you," he interrupts me as he slips the manilla folder from my arms and stuffs it into the leather briefcase he's carrying. "You're a godsend."

His eyes are lingering long with mine now, sending curls of desire through my belly. I still can't tell if he recognizes me from *before*. I thought maybe the red lips or the short dress would trigger some long-buried memory but maybe it's better that it doesn't. It's not what I'm here for after all — I'm here to prove that his secret is *me* — at least it needs to look that way to Gen. And anyway, if I play this right it's not like it will even be a lie. Chemistry still thrums between us like a heartbeat — that's undeniable.

"How was your drive?" His voice is deep. I didn't realize how much I missed it until that moment.

"Quick," I reply. I'm not exactly experienced with men — my flirting skills are awkward at best and at the moment the only thing running through my mind is something my dad always said: a woman should be seen and not heard. I suppress a groan. He must think the new au pair is about as entertaining as being stuck in rush hour traffic. If this is going to work I'll have to at least *pretend* to be charming and friendly to this man. And if he realizes we have a past history? I'll claim ignorance — that it was pure happenstance that I bumped into his wife that day at the school.

It wasn't of course, but that's another story.

The doors of the elevator open then and Alex gestures for me to exit first. As I do I feel the barest touch of his palm hovering at the small of my back. A shiver of awareness runs through me.

"Are you hungry? I have reservations in Little Havana but I understand if you're in a hurry to get back to Palm Beach." Alex is a perfect gentleman as he guides me down the hallway.

"I'm starving. And why waste a perfectly pretty little black dress?" I smile up at him.

He opens the door of the apartment and drops his brief-case and the file just inside the door before he turns to take me in again. His grin tips sideways. "That dress is more than a *little* pretty." His eyes gleam as his palms hover at my elbows. "Are you trying to drive me crazy?"

I shake my head, tongue lodged in my throat.

"Well, you are." He leans closer, the tickle of his breath on my skin sends shivers through me. "It'll be just like old times, huh, *Sugar?*"

And there it is.

The moment I've been dancing around. *Does he remember or does he not?*

"I didn't think you remembered," I stutter.

"How could I forget?" He drags a fingertip along the shell of my ear and down the line of my throat. "That night was so hot — the music and the mojitos. Little Havana isn't ready for us."

My voice is wistful as I get lost in the memory. "I think we ended up on the beach at dawn."

He groans softly, like he's lost in another time with me. "It's one of my favorite memories — sand, sun, and *me* on your skin."

I didn't expect this. I didn't imagine Alex would be so eager to spend time with me again, but then, why wouldn't he be? He's happy to live a life away from his wife and family all week — isn't this what Gen suspected? That he had lovers in Miami that kept him occupied and disinterested in her? I'm just here to prove her hunch is right, and if Alex leaves his wife and we finally get our happily-ever-after? Well, then that's just the cherry on top of the sundae. Does that make me a homewrecker? Hardly — I'm just willing to offer up the evidence this woman needs to get the divorce they're clearly headed for. A split is on the horizon for the Moreau-DuPont family. I'm here to make sure of it.

"Ready to paint the town, beautiful?" He drags his finger-tips along my arms and shivers course through me in his wake.

"I was born ready." I breathe against his neck. "I've missed this."

"Me too." He grins. "Where have you been all my life?"

"Right under your nose," I tease. But really though — I've been right here, within a few dozen miles of him all this time. I wish he'd looked me up — but a fish needs bait before it bites. So here I am, baiting him with my little black dress and heels. I can't get caught up in what could have been. I'm here now, that's all that matters.

An hour later we're sitting at a two-person café table in a dimly lit Cuban restaurant drinking mojitos and laughing, just like old times. I feel super-charged with confidence as I realize this man still wants me — at least if the hand that's been caressing my bare thigh under the table is any indication. My nipples are hard and my breaths are growing more shallow with each passing caress. Alex has always been a man who gets what he wants — even six years ago when we were last together — I was helpless to his advances.

"I've been thinking . . ." he says as he finishes his third mojito. "Would you kill me if I said we should do this every week?" He speaks quietly, as if he's just proposed something downright scandalous. "I like being here with you. The firm is breathing down my neck to revise the blueprints on this Flamingo Bay building because the investors are — well, never mind. It's just . . . I forgot what this feels like. Hell, sometimes I think I've lost myself to this life."

His admission hits home.

I don't imagine I could be the one he's looking for — so upside down and opposite from his own wife, but maybe, just maybe I'm exactly what he needs. His life in Palm Beach is so pretentious and predictable — but downtown and far away from the pearls and PTA meetings we can just be two people that enjoy each other again.

The waiter arrives then, offering another round of booze.

"I think we're good—" Alex glances at me, "are you ready to get out of here?" I nod. His palm squeezes my knee and then he nods at the waiter. "We'll take the check, please."

Minutes later we're walking in the opposite direction of Alex's apartment toward the beach. My hand has found its way into his and I would be lying if I said just the smallest touch didn't light me on fire.

"We should get a hotel on the beach for the night." His husky tone breaks me from my haze.

"I–I—" I stammer as my mind sizzles with his offer. I didn't expect this — can I really sleep with a married man? It certainly seems like he's ready for whatever might happen. "I should get back — I'll be dragging at school drop-off tomorrow."

He pauses and turns me to him, palms cupping my cheeks. "I've always thought you were incredible. I have so many regrets these last five years. I know this situation isn't typical and I would understand if this is all too much — but it would mean the world to me if we could do this again."

I pause, our gazes lingering as I fall into the possibility of us.

Things were flawless when we were together — at least I thought so. Until I woke up one day to a stranger — he stopped answering my calls and refused to acknowledge me on social media. Just like that, we were done. I never had any closure — and now I know why — because of *her.*

"Okay," I finally say, unsure of what I've just agreed to. Anxiety ripples to life in my veins. This is too much, too soon. I've only just moved into the Moreau-DuPont estate and already I'm willing to fall into bed with the man of the house.

A young Cuban couple steps out of a restaurant, salsa music chugging through the thick air around them before the man circles her slim waist with his arm and draws her close to him. They kiss passionately before their bodies begin to move in a rhythm all their own. Their steps follow the music, but instead of spinning her at arm's length as the dance steps normally do, he wraps her in his arms and kisses her in a fashion I'm sure that I've never been kissed. With one hand wrapped around her waist and the other holding her to him by the neck, he kisses her like he's drawing the oxygen from her lungs.

"I'm turned on just watching them," I confess.

Alex murmurs something I can't make out before he spins me in his arms and then with sensual precision, slides an open palm from my thigh, over the dip of my waist, all the way to the soft hollow of my throat. He pulls me closer in just the way the other man did, and then our lips lock. And he does steal my breath.

In one quick instant, all that has separated us these last six years vanishes. I am his again.

CHAPTER SIXTEEN

"Hey, Sugar." Alex *plants a kiss on my knuckles before sweeping me into his arms and pressing another to my lips.*

"Mm, hi . . ." I breathe into him. It's our third date in the week since we met but we've been talking every single day, sometimes for hours.

"You're beautiful," he murmurs. "Thanks for seeing me."

"I love seeing you," I coo back and wrap my arms around his waist. We walk into the private room at the fanciest hotel downtown — I know because I searched it on the internet before I got here. Alex offered to pick me up like a perfect gentleman, but I slipped up on the first day we met and told him I live in Palm Beach. It's not totally a lie — I did stay there for a few days when I first arrived from Pahokee, but I don't technically have a permanent residence that he could easily pick me up at in Palm Beach. So what's one little white lie?

Anyway, if I told him the truth . . . well, he'd run the other way. A man like Alex wouldn't be caught dead with a girl like me. Men like Alexandre Moreau-DuPont don't marry girls from Pahokee. And I've put too much work into this one already. This one is good. I need this one to work out.

A chill slides up my spine as an unwanted memory flashes through my skull.

My first night in Palm Beach. The women's shelter. The man that gave me my first job and changed my life. And also ruined it.

Alex smiles at me. His eyes are doing this sparkling thing that tells me that he's hooked. It's not the first time I've seen this kind of lust-struck gaze, but hopefully it's the last. I'm adept at the needs of men — stroke their ego, make them feel like they're in charge and you're an innocent bird in need of protection, and then blow their minds between the sheets. Alex hasn't even been to second base yet — the most we've done is kiss. I need to play sexy but coy, every message and every meeting is a dance that keeps him on tenterhooks, and the more energy he puts into wooing me the harder it will be for him to walk away.

Taking care of weak men is my superpower — they're the easiest to hook. But Alex isn't weak. He's powerful and successful. The perfect good-on-paper guy. He's just the kind of challenge I need right now.

"Bar or booth, Sugar?" Alex pulls me a little closer as the host at the Japanese steakhouse waits for our answer.

"Whatever you want," I gleam back at him.

"Give us a booth," he says to the host, then threads his fingers at the base of my neck and nips at my ear once. "I'd eat you up right here if they'd let me."

His words send tendrils of warmth through my body. "You're so naughty."

A groan vibrates through his chest when I slide into the booth, grazing the front of his trousers with my bottom as I do. "You're so sexy."

"That makes two of us on the crazy train then," I say once he's next to me. My palm lingers on his thigh briefly.

"You should stay the night at my place tonight," he says before he's even picked up the drink menu.

"Oh yeah?" I tease.

He nods. His palm is on my thigh. Fireworks are lighting inside of me. "Say yes. I promise you won't regret it."

His words snap me back to a memory I haven't thought of in years.

My father pushing me into the arms of his best friend. Sweaty hands crawling over my skin. Whisky breath on my neck. Dingy ceiling tiles, brown with water-stains as fingers the size of sausages violate me. Lights out. A strange, black emptiness consumes me as I fade to black.

"Whaddya say, Sugar?" Alex's baritone shakes me into the present.

"Yes. Yes. That sounds perfect." I plaster the smile he's expecting on my face. I will never let this man see the darkness that lurks just beneath the surface of me. If he did, he'd leave. They always leave. I am trouble, wild and unpredictable, some days it feels like my mind is lit with fire, singed at the edges as the past and present collide.

If Alex knew how dark the darkness was for me, he'd never speak to me again.

I think back to the morning ten days ago when I sat in last night's little black dress, alone in a strange penthouse, searching the internet for Miami-based Fortune 500 companies.

Alex thinks our meeting that day at the hospital was a chance meeting, but the truth remains that I had my sights on Alexandre Moreau-DuPont for weeks in advance. I knew he was an up-and-coming architect, and I knew his biggest job to date was the new addition of Trinity Medical Hospital. Alex has spent every day at Trinity for the last month. It's the first place he stops in the morning, coffee in hand to confer with the building team, and it's where he spends most of his lunchtime, going over plans and finalizing details for the day.

Alex thinks he bumped into me that day.

Alex thinks he's in control of this thing between us.

But what Alex doesn't know won't hurt him.

CHAPTER SEVENTEEN

Genevieve

"Late night?" I take in Adeline's tired eyes, last night's mascara still smudged under the lash line.

"I got home around midnight," she states simply.

"Mm." I clear my throat as a dozen conflicting feelings rush through me. "Where did you go?"

"Miami to meet friends."

"Surprised you didn't run into my husband while you were there." I know I'm being snide but I'm annoyed that she ran off to Miami last night without a word. It's not like she's a prisoner to this place, she can leave whenever she chooses, but the responsible thing would be to at least tell your employer before you dart off to Miami for a night out. "I'm glad you feel comfortable enough to make yourself at home here, but please, next time just give me a head's up before you leave."

"Of course," she replies.

I hate how little she speaks. All of her one-word answers leave me with more questions. I find myself wanting to fill the silence and that usually leaves me with the sense that I've revealed too much. This woman is a stranger, I remind myself.

But then, maybe her anonymity is exactly the reason I feel comfortable enough to air my deepest and darkest thoughts.

"I had a meeting with a divorce attorney this week." I throw into the void. It's the first time I've allowed myself to say this out loud. The word divorce on my lips is foreign. I don't know if I'm ready, but I don't think I'll ever know as long as I keep it to myself. Adeline is safe, so I decide to reveal more.

"Oh?" She doesn't seem to be paying any attention to me as she wipes down the stovetop after making eggs and bacon for the children. "Have you spoken to Mr. DuPont?"

"No — of course not." I settle myself at the kitchen counter and watch her work.

"Do you really think he's seeing someone else in Miami during the week?"

"What else would I think? He's so checked out — even when he's here. I noticed last weekend that he sets his phone face down on the counter whenever he's in the room with me. Maybe it's nothing, but maybe not. He never allows Albertine to play with his phone so she's always on mine playing games. And when I ask him how his week was, he always replies with the same thing: *Fine*. That's it. Just *fine*. He was always so open before he started working in Miami, now he's just avoidant and evasive and downright dismissive of me."

"He does seem distracted when he's here." Comes her tentative reply.

"I just can't help but think he's getting his needs met elsewhere." A ball of emotion settles in my throat as I say the words out loud. "The attorney I met with is the best in Palm Beach — Melinda recommended her after she left Bill." I frown, thinking about the steep hourly rate she's charging but it will be worth it if it means keeping the money I earned before Alex and I were married. "If I can prove he's cheating, the pre-nup will be broken. I won't have to pay him a dime and we can just go our separate ways. We can pretend this marriage never happened." Pain swirls in my stomach. "God, it's so sad to say it out loud. Six years of marriage flushed down the toilet. I never thought a divorce would be in the cards for me."

"Is that what you want, Ms.?" Adeline asks.

"I . . . don't know. It's hard pouring so much love into someone that won't love you back. I can't do it forever." I press my lips together so tightly they begin to throb. "Sometimes I think the slowest way to kill someone is to withhold love. We connected so easily in the beginning, so why does it feel like we're strangers now?" I wince with the pain of the words. I push a hand over my face, feeling every bit of my thirty-four years this morning. Laurent woke me up in tears with a soaked crib and Albertine took my favorite pair of diamond studs from the bathroom counter for Puppy to play with but now she's forgotten where Puppy left them. I have half a mind to throw Puppy in the garbage disposal and threaten to maim him if she doesn't tell me where my diamonds are, but I have a feeling that'll only make matters worse. And she'll tell Alexandre. Something like despair settles on my shoulders.

"Is Mr. DuPont coming home today?" Adeline asks.

"Of course. It's Friday. Why wouldn't he?" I shoot back.

"I just . . . I don't know." Adeline's reply comes in a whisper.

"He should be home around four — just like every Friday." I dig through my bag in search of my keys. "Do you know where the keys for the Audi are?"

"They should be on the key rack, Ms.," Adeline says softly as she pulls carrots out of the fridge. I've asked her to restock the frozen baby food — this is an all-day project and one that often overwhelmed me while taking care of the children at the same time but I have faith that Adeline can handle it. She's more capable — at least at this moment. I have a hundred things on my mind and none of them are related to the care and keeping of Laurent and Albertine.

I feel bad for caving and hiring an au pair — I always said I wouldn't be one of those women who has children only to have someone else raise them. But I could never predict a time such as this — when my husband would spend all week in Miami while I languish poolside and try to determine the exact moment things went sideways for us.

"Well, I have to get on with my day. So many errands, so little time, right?" I force a cheery smile. "The pharmacist is having issues filling our prescriptions — Alex needs his sleeping medication and Albertine is out of her inhaler and if I don't get my anxiety meds soon I might have a bona fide breakdown. A mom can only handle so much, ya know?" I chuckle like I'm kidding. The truth is I wish I was. I've been giving everything I have lately — it's killing me and yet it's still not enough. "I'll pick up some squash, peas, and avocados — those are Laurent's favorites. We can have a whole day of baby food making!"

"Sounds perfect, Ms.," comes Adeline's reply.

Albertine runs into the kitchen, her screams bouncing off the cathedral ceilings like she's on fire. "Maman! Can I come too?"

"Not this time, baby." I pat her on the head. Her eyes narrow and something hateful seems to possess her before she clutches one of my teardrop earrings in her little fist and yanks. I yelp as pain throbs through my earlobe. She holds my earring up in her hand, tiny drops of blood clinging to her fist.

"Albertine!" I finally manage to gasp. I pull my hand from my earlobe and find fresh blood. I shoot across the kitchen and swipe a paper towel to press to my ear. "I can't believe you just did that. You hurt Maman!"

She pouts, narrows her eyes at me and then bursts into tears. It takes every ounce of patience in me not to spank her with the nearest thing within reach. I promised myself I would never hit my children, but there are some days I think it's exactly what they need.

"Adeline — *please?*" I beg, because I don't know how to get Albertine to stop this tantrum.

Adeline nods and rushes to my daughter's side. She wraps her in a warm hug, pats her back and slides a palm down her shiny hair. She's motherly and nurturing and everything I am not. A pit of jealousy forms in my stomach.

Adeline is the kind of woman that's probably fulfilled by motherhood.

And here I am, trying to run out the back door.

CHAPTER EIGHTEEN

Adeline

"Albertine — honey, please," I beg. She's been on edge all day, from willful to tearful at a moment's notice. Albertine has also become clingy in the last few days — there's no doubt that she senses that Gen is disconnected. It makes me sad that she's looking to me to be a mother figure but I'm the last person that should be trusted with kids. I've never been an au pair in my life but when an opportunity presents itself, I don't sleep on it.

Albertine has been helping me in the kitchen, scooping pureed carrots into small jars that we'll freeze for Laurent in between her alligator tears. This child is going through something, but who isn't in this house? Just as we're sealing the last jar of baby food, the garage door swings open.

"Daddy!" Albertine runs down the hallway and right into the arms of her dad. His eyes dash across the kitchen to meet mine for a beat and then flicker away again.

"Hey, baby girl." He lifts and swings her around before planting kisses on her ruddy cheeks. "Have you been crying?"

"Maman's mean to me." Albertine sucks up her tears.

"I'm sure she didn't mean it, baby." His voice is deep and measured. The memory of his words in my ear last night sends a sensual thrill through me. "Whaddya say you help me unpack my bags?"

I hear Albertine sniff and then murmur, "Okay."

Silence hangs in the kitchen for the first time in an hour. Albertine's mood swings from joyous and cheery to wild and willful, and she's always so damn loud. I'm finding she's best in small doses — all kids are, really. Parenthood is the only job you can't resign from — there are no take backs or redoes and it would seem that Gen is desperately seeking either one. When I was hired as the au pair I anticipated taking care of the kids, what I didn't anticipate was being the stand-in for their mother. With their dad gone all week in Miami and Gen practically divorced from reality, I'm left to juggle all the pieces.

I finish cleaning up the kitchen and then return to the pool house. The little black dress I wore last night still hangs on a bathroom hook. I wrap it in my arms and bring the soft fabric to my nose and inhale — it still smells like his cologne with notes of tobacco and leather. He's been wearing this same cologne for as long as I've known him — I'm the one that introduced him to it when I gave it to him as a gift for his birthday when we were together. It brings a smile to my face that he still wears it now.

I'll need to wash the dress before I hang it back in Gen's closet, but a part of me wants to leave it just like this; maybe curl up in it while I sleep and pretend it's him that's wrapped around me and not just his scent. And then a thought occurs to me, I can use this to my advantage. I spritz my Creed perfume sampler in the air and then wave my undergarments from last night through the scented plume. A diabolical grin splits my lips as I ball the garments in my hands and then move quickly out of the pool house and across the back patio. I listen intently as I reach the back door, trying to locate where Albertine and Alex might be. I hear her little bird song voice prattling to him in her playroom upstairs, so I head down the hallway that leads to Alex's office. Because the laundry is located nearby, I've noticed this is where he brings his luggage before he unpacks and washes it.

I locate the navy and leather trimmed duffle that belongs to him and quickly tuck my things deep inside.

There. A satisfied smile turns my lips as I climb the stairs. I don't even feel guilt for this little trick because it only proves Gen's worst fear — that her husband is a cheating letch. Gen has a right to know the kind of man she married — he's been hiding who he is — pretending to be someone else all week. When Alex is in Miami, he is far from the loving family man he pretends to be — I'm just committed to revealing the truth to his devoted wife. While she carries the weight of motherhood on her shoulders all week, he's salsa dancing with beautiful women on the streets of Little Havana.

A painful memory flickers like a dying lightbulb in my mind. The echoes of my past are just that — faint remembrances that haunt the ether of my consciousness, their edges undefined and blurred as I struggle to parse fact from fiction so many years later. There is much about my father that I have chosen to forget since I left, but the overall feeling that remains is that trust should be earned and not given, and that few men have the capacity to give more than they receive. And even fewer are worthy of the trust women place in them. My father was an example of that every day of my life — and now, so is Alex.

I'm lost in my thoughts as I move down the main floor hallway in the direction of the kitchen. The kids will want lunch soon; I know Gen likes to encourage Albertine to make her own sandwiches for lunchtime, but I feel bad that the little girl eats cold lunches all week long. Just as I decide to make homemade macaroni and cheese for a special lunch, the door from the garage swings wide and Gen's clickity-clackity heels echo around the main floor.

"Oh!" Gen plants a hand across her chest. "You scared me — why are you always sneaking around? It's so . . . creepy."

She huffs like she's just made a joke but it's not funny at all — she's the one that asked me *not to be seen or heard* and now she's complaining that I'm doing my job too well? "I'm famished!" Gen says after setting her bag down on the kitchen island. "Whaddya say we have baked potatoes with escargot for lunch? The other wives at the country club get it all the time — it sounds weird, but it's delicious, trust me." Her eyes swing across the kitchen to catch mine. "You'll have some, right?"

"Ugh," I stir the slow-simmering cheese sauce in the pot, "sure."

"Perfect." Gen pulls two potatoes from the bin and then turns the oven on to preheat. I notice the tiny tear in her right earlobe from Albertine. I have to fight the small smile that threatens my lips. "How do you feel now that you're settling in?"

"Oh, perfectly well. Albertine is so precious," the lie falls off my lips easily. In reality, the kid can be a holy terror, but who wouldn't be with a mom like Gen? "I feel so lucky to have bumped into you that day at school pickup — like we were meant to find each other," I double down on my lies.

"I couldn't agree more." She stabs the potatoes with a knife so viciously it makes me cringe. "You're like the sister I never had — I truly feel that way."

"Me too, Ms.," I smile sweetly. "Just like soul sisters."

Gen slides the potatoes in the oven and then closes the door and settles herself at the island. "You didn't notice anything odd about Alexandre earlier, did you?"

"No. Why?"

"He just rushed out to the club to play golf so quickly I didn't even get a chance to talk to him."

"I suppose he did seem distracted." I add fuel to her fears, faking a sympathetic frown. Is it me he's trying to avoid?

Her gaze falls to her hands. "I'm sure he'll be gone until late tonight — golf is never just golf, ya know? It's eighteen holes with the boys, and then dinner and drinks and — well,

I can't help but think maybe he's not even golfing at all." She sighs. "I've been trying to trust my instincts more, but . . . what if they're wrong and I destroy a marriage? And then I think . . . well, what if that's what I want? Maybe I was never supposed to be a mother or a wife, it's always felt so foreign to me. I don't fit in at the country club, I don't fit in with the other partner's wives at Alexandre's firm, I certainly don't fit with the other wives in the neighborhood. I feel like a failure, to be honest. When Alexandre asked me to marry him it was all such a dream come true, but no one talks about what happens after happily-ever-after. What if my *ever after* isn't happy? What if I chose all wrong and I'm going to ruin things?"

"Ms.—" I turn down the simmering sauce before pouring it over the cooked macaroni waiting in the casserole dish, "maybe this is just a tough season. The kids are young and—"

"No, no this isn't that." Gen leans closer as if she's about to tell me a secret. "Since the day Alexandre asked me to marry him I've been wondering if *I do* was the worst mistake of my life. Alexandre and I haven't been the same since. What if . . . what if marriage isn't a blessing but a curse?"

My heart beats wildly as I think about how close this woman is to walking out the door forever. A split in the Moreau-DuPont household feels imminent.

"How could I get it so wrong, ya know? It's like I didn't know myself and just . . . went with the flow."

I swallow the ball of resentment in my throat that this woman is throwing away everything I would be so grateful to have. She still doesn't know what she's doing and I suddenly see why it is her husband would rather spend all week away from her — she's indecisive and spoiled and downright neglectful.

"I just wish he'd want me again. I wish we could be like we were and then maybe we'd have a shot at a family but like this . . ." she shakes her head.

"A lot of men work away all week — it's just a matter of cherishing the time you do have together. Have you told him how you feel?"

"He's arrogant and dismissive — just says he's tired from work all week, *what do I expect him to do?*" She mocks his stern tone.

"Well, have you tried showing him how you feel?"

"Showing him? What do you mean?" Gen looks genuinely confused about how to show love to her husband.

"Well, I saw his unpacked luggage in his office when I was cleaning — maybe you could do his laundry or—"

"Oh! That's a great idea." Gen hops up from the barstool. "Maybe if I do what I can to make his life easier he'll have more time to spend with me, cherish me more — like you said."

Did I say that? I suppress an eyeroll. This woman hears what she wants to hear and nothing more.

"Men love to be nurtured," I confirm.

"Yes, maybe it's that simple. I've been so wrapped up with the children the last few months that's probably something I've let slide." Her eyes shift from me to the macaroni and cheese I'm assembling and then she laughs, "it's not like I'd want *you* poking around in his things anyway, right?"

A saccharin smile turns my lips. "Right."

CHAPTER NINETEEN

"Morning, Sugar." His gravelly morning voice sends delicious shivers through my veins.

"Hi." I grin sweetly up at him. Alex and I have been living together for three months and somehow, every day is better than the last. With him I've found something I didn't know was possible — a calm sense of belonging. His touch soothes me in some moments and drives me wild with passion in others. We're magic, him and I, and I'll do whatever it takes to make sure he never wants me to leave.

"It's nearly noon. Guess we had a late night last night," he swats at my bare bottom as I climb out of our cozy, sun-soaked king bed. Alex rented us a charming, 1930s bungalow in the heart of Miami. Nestled among bodegas and Cuban restaurants, we found love. I'm fully aware that we are living in a love bubble that won't last forever— but I'll make sure it lasts as long as I need. "You want me to order-in breakfast?"

I nod, blowing him a kiss before I enter the en suite bathroom. A moment later I'm finished and washing my hands when the doorbell sounds through the house.

"Wonder who that is." Alex moves to push himself from the bed.

"I got it — you stay. And don't you dare put on any clothes! I'll be right back." I stick out my tongue playfully before pulling a cotton robe around my shoulders and leaving our bedroom. The doorbell buzzes again and I can tell that whoever is on the other side of the door is getting impatient.

"Coming," I grumble, tightening the belt of the robe as I swing the door open.

"Hi, Baby."

"What. The. Fuck?" I slam the door closed as quickly as I opened it. The next knock is louder.

What the fuck am I going to do? I suck in a breath, attempting to control the anger threatening to split me in half. He knocks again.

"Argh." I growl, opening the door and sliding out into the warm Florida sunshine. "Dad."

"Baby — I'm so glad I tracked you down."

"I'm not," I grit.

He continues, as if I haven't said a thing. He's always been like this — like I'm only a hologram in his reality — a projection that isn't a thinking feeling human but just someone he can use and discard when it works for him. "I can't believe you've been right here this entire time. Just under my nose." He leans in to pinch my nose like he used to when I was a kid. A cloud of whisky breath chokes me.

I dodge his gesture. "Why are you here?"

"To see my girl—"

"Stop. Please. Make this quick. I have plans." I'm rattled. I have to get this man off of my porch before Alex joins us in this little reunion.

"I thought we could catch up—"

"No."

"I thought we could—"

"No." I cross my arms. "Tell me why you're really here."

My father rubs a palm over his face. He hasn't had a shave in weeks, his eyes are glassy and unfocused, if I had to bet I'd say he's not just drunk but high too. "I need help — just a few thousand to get me out of the shelter—"

"No. You always need help. I can't help you. Please, don't come back." I make a move to go back inside but he clamps down on my arm with a heavy palm. An ice bath floods my system as my stomach drops.

"Don't. Touch. Me." I seethe as I tear my arm from his grip.

His eyes round before the cold, hard gaze I grew up with falls on me. "I know your boyfriend has money. I know who he is and where he works and I know he buys you all this fancy shit. You may be a fucking

95

city girl now but I won't let you forget where you came from. How could you forget who raised you, girl? I gave up everything—"

"No you didn't. You didn't give up anything. You allowed me to live in a house with you and your drug addict friends and you let them use me for drugs. You let them—" I catch myself, pulling back on the overwhelming emotions before I descend into a rage spiral. I sigh, gathering myself. "You need to leave now."

With that I leave the piece-of-shit that raised me on the front porch, locking the door behind me once I'm safely in.

Every fiber of my being wants to run.

Instead, I compose myself and walk back down the hallway to Alex. Right before I reach the closed bedroom door, it swings wide and there he is, the man of my dreams.

"Aw, you got dressed." I frown as I take in the boxer briefs clinging to his hips.

He chuckles, wraps me in a hug and plants a kiss on my forehead. "I ordered breakfast from that café down the street. I got you the blueberry pancakes you love."

"Thanks." I breathe, holding back tears. This man makes me feel so safe, so worthy, so doted on that I would do anything to keep him.

"Who was at the door?" Alex pulls away and moves into the kitchen.

"Oh, just a sad homeless guy. I gave him a few bucks to go away," I utter. "A morning drunk, the worst kind."

"That's sad." Alex pours two glasses of orange juice. "You're good to give him anything — people like that create their own trouble."

I nod. "So much trouble." I lift the orange juice and sip. "I hope he doesn't come back."

CHAPTER TWENTY

Genevieve

"Babe!" Alexandre's voice booms up the stairs. I consider not answering him — it wouldn't be the first time I pretended to be asleep just to avoid a conversation. "You up there?"

I groan, push myself out of bed and straighten my hair in the mirror taking extra care to make sure my hair hangs in just the right way to disguise my bald spot. "I'm here!"

His steps come two at a time up the stairs and within thirty seconds he's entering our bedroom. "Hey."

"Hey." I wrap him in a hug. He tucks my head under his chin and slides an open palm down my hair. His embrace is comforting, but I would be lying if I said it didn't feel a little off. I can't shake the feeling that he's been unfaithful — he's had so much opportunity these last months and we've been so very broken lately.

"You feeling okay?" he murmurs. He's always been so in-tune with my moods, I could never hide anything from this man. But I can't help but wonder how good *he* is at hiding things from me.

"I'm feeling okay, I guess," I finally reply.

"Well, I've been thinking we need a little getaway so I booked us a night at The Breakers. I'll play a little golf, you can have a spa day, we'll have some great food — I heard they have a new executive chef that's not to be missed."

"When?" I ask.

"Tomorrow. You think you can get the nanny to watch the kids overnight on such short notice?"

"Yeah, of course. She's great," I utter, mind spinning. Alexandre never plans dates or special weekends for us — that part of our relationship has always been up to me. Apparently until now. It's almost like he feels guilty for something. I do my best to strike the thought from my mind — I want to enjoy this night away with my husband. It might be our last.

He cups my cheeks and plants a gentle kiss on my lips. "We have such a good life. I know it's not always sunshine and roses."

Emotion overwhelms me as I let his words sink in. Then why hasn't it felt good in so long? Guilt washes through me for meeting with a divorce attorney this past week, but I only needed to know my options. Just because I took a meeting doesn't mean anything. Does it?

"We've been through a lot together," Alexandre whispers, emotion threading his tone. All I can do is nod. "So," he pulls away and swats my bottom playfully, "pack your prettiest dress and your smallest bikini — we're gonna pretend we're young again — just like old times, right?"

His grin tips sideways and for the first time in so long, a few butterflies flutter to life behind my ribcage.

"Right," I say before he turns and walks out the door.

And then, the tiniest seed of hope is planted inside of me that maybe this isn't over. Maybe we *aren't* headed for a split. Maybe we've only just begun.

"I guess I need to pack," I say to myself, heading to my bureau to pull out my favorite tiny black and gold bikini. I toss it on the bed and then move to the walk-in and locate my beach cover-up and an overnight bag. I take them to the bed and then think about the fact that I never did throw Alexandre's laundry into the wash like I'd planned to do earlier. Feeling a little lighter at the thought of doing something for my husband in an effort to show him I care, I leave my room and head to the lower level in search of the bag he brings to Miami every week.

I find it right where he always leaves it when he gets home — just inside the door of his office waiting to be unpacked and laundered. I pick it up and take it directly into the laundry room and toss all of it into the washing machine. I throw a detergent pod on the top of the pile of dirty clothes and it's then that I notice it's not just Alexandre's things I'm about to wash.

Scooping a pile of black satin in my hands, I bring it to my nose and inhale. The strong scent of floral perfume clings to the fabric. I shake out the garments and the tiniest black thong and push-up bra tumbles out.

I shudder when I realize what this is.

Proof.

CHAPTER TWENTY-ONE

Adeline

"I want to watch *Christmas Chronicles* by the pool!" Albertine shouts at the top of her little lungs.

"Ugh. Really?" I practically growl back.

She squints and crosses her arms like a little boss bitch. I'm afraid of her, I am — but only because I can't afford to have her hate me. I sense that Gen is reaching a point of no return — last week a divorce attorney, this week a strange woman's underwear in his luggage. I just need another week or two tops and I know Gen will be filing divorce papers.

"I. Want. To. Watch—" Albertine is stomping her ballet-slippered foot with every word.

"Oh my God. Okay. Okay. How do we watch it outside?"

"Daddy keeps the movies in the pool house! You just have to point the movie player thingy at the wall and hit play!" She's skipping down the hallway and straight out the back door to the pool area.

It's already after sunset and Gen and Alex have been gone all day — I'm exhausted keeping Albertine happy and Laurent fed and clean around the clock. I wish I could put them to bed early and be done with it but Albertine has another two hours before bedtime, so I guess setting her up with a movie is my best option if I want a little peace and quiet.

"You have to make popcorn too — the extra buttery kind!" Albertine throws the pool house door open wide and runs to the chest that sits in the center of the living area. She opens the top and then points at a small movie projector. "You pick it up and I'll show you where Daddy puts it."

I nod, carrying it back out the door as I trail after her. She points to the outdoor bar and then spins and throws herself into the nearest pool lounger. I adjust the projector to aim it towards the whitewashed wall of the pool house. "See! Now you just push play!"

Albertine is practically giddy — she's so sweet when she's happy and practically the devil's spawn when she's not. This kid could use a heavier hand — my dad firmly believed in the old adage: *spare the rod, spoil the child*. If the kitchen wasn't cleaned to his liking or if I got anything less than a B on a test at school — I was punished in a variety of clever ways. The belt was his favorite because it was always close by, but he also liked psychological torture as much as physical. I shudder as I think about the girl Albertine might've grown into had she been raised by someone like my father and less like her own.

"Popcorn!" Albertine yells as the opening credits roll on the Christmas movie she requested.

"Fine. Give me five minutes." I spit at her but she's already ignoring me.

I head back to the kitchen just as Laurent lets out a howl.

"Fuck. *Me."* My frustration is turning to a slow-simmering rage. I climb the stairs following the sound of the little boy's cries. He must be wet, or worse. By the time I get him bathed and ready for bed he'll want to eat something and Albertine will be livid without her *extra* buttery popcorn if it's not in her lap in the next twelve seconds.

No wonder Gen hates these kids. They're positively unbearable. Always wanting and needing and *crying, crying, crying.*

I reluctantly lift the chubby little shit from his crib and spend the next two minutes changing his diaper and fighting with him to stay in one place.

"If you were my fucking kid you'd be potty-trained by now." I hiss at him. It seems to distract him, because he stops, eyes as round as saucers as he takes me in. I finish diaper clean-up and pull him into my arms just as Albertine screams like the holy terror she is.

I don't even reply to her, only stomp down the stairs with the squirming baby in my arms and shoot her a death glare. Her own evil stare matches mine in intensity. "Popcorn."

I snarl at her but follow her on quick steps out to the pool area. She's already hauled the little theater popcorn maker out along with the bag of popcorn and gross buttery sauce. "Can I push start?"

"Sure, hit it," I say and she does. The popcorn machine begins to hum and Albertine settles back on the lounger peacefully.

"Why are you even here? I don't need you. I can make my own food." A smug smile spreads Albertine's face. It takes everything in me not to shove her off the lounger and stick out my tongue just to see what she'd do.

"You know what, Albertine? If you were my kid I'd send you to boarding school. *Forever.*" I know it's petty — but so is she and this kid could use a lesson or two about the real world.

She scrunches her nose at me. "What's boarding school?"

"Hell," I grit.

"What's hell?" She chirps.

I huff, realizing I'll never win. Laurent squirms in my arms, his eyes riveted on the flying reindeer in the movie.

"Keep an eye on him while I go get some baby food, okay?" I settle him on the lounger between her legs.

Albertine nods. Laurent isn't quite walking yet, so I'm not really worried about him getting away very fast. I can heat up some baby food in the microwave and be back out here in under a minute. What trouble could the little freeloaders get into while I'm gone? They're practically zombies for Santa Claus and his reindeer right now.

I seize the moment of peace and head back to the main house to get food for the baby. I pull carrots and peas from the freezer and make quick work of heating them in the microwave. I take another minute and grab warm oat milk for him. Gen insists on organic and sustainable everything, just like the other members of the mommy cult, I'm sure. In Palm Beach, perception is everything and what happens behind closed doors is of little matter. I pile everything I need onto a serving tray, including spoons, napkins, and organic apple juice for Albertine and head back to the pool. But as soon as I reach the back door I know something is very wrong.

Albertine is walking around the edge of the pool and her brother is nowhere to be found.

Once she notices me coming closer, she looks up at me with big brown eyes and then cries, "I'm sorry!"

"For what?" I set the tray down on the nearest lounger and go to her.

I drop to my knees, plant my hands on her shoulders and shake her softly. "Honey — what happened?"

She sniffs and wipes at tears running down her cheeks. "I lost him."

"Where did he go?" I ask, eyes scanning the patio and pool.

She only shrugs. "I was watching the movie. It was my favorite part."

I want to yell and scream and slap her across the face for her selfishness but I don't have time.

"Laurent!" I shout into the dim light. The pool is lit in shades of green and blue but the rest of the patio and pool area is shrouded in shadow. "Laurent!"

Albertine begins to call into the night air before she darts off towards the back patio. "The gate is open!"

"What?" I shout as I rush to where she's standing. She's right, from far away the gate looks like it's closed and latched but it's not — it's cracked just wide enough for a fat little baby to crawl his way through. "Albertine — did you see him come this way?"

She shakes her head. "I don't know."

I growl in frustration. I scan the pool and patio area one more time to confirm he's not there. I push through the gate and move down the dark path in the direction of the small waterway that splits this estate from the next. If he's out here there's no way he crawled away from the path — tall damp grass lines either side. It's less than ten yards from the back gate to the waterway.

"Laurent!" I call into the night. Albertine is fast on my heels and shouting into the air too. I reach the shores and take in the scene — moonlight glinting off the small ripples and no crawling baby anywhere to be seen.

"Do you think he fell in?" Albertine says the one thing I've been trying to avoid thinking.

"I don't know," I whisper.

I suck in a breath, kick off my shoes, and then take a few steps into the warm water. The bottom is thick with muck and my feet nearly get stuck with every step.

"Watch out for alligators!" Albertine screams.

"I know, I know." Tears slide down my cheeks as I search. How could a child vanish in the span of a breath? I was only gone for two minutes at most, wasn't I?

Albertine is running up and down the shoreline screaming for her brother. I can't focus on anything. All I can hear is the unbearable roar of my own heartbeat. The whoosh of the wind through the reeds. The slapping water against the muddy shore. Albertine *screaming, screaming, screaming.* "Shut up!" I wail into the dark night. "Albertine, please — shut up!"

She freezes at the shore, her eyes wide and wild on me. Her hair is a tangle around her face and tears are streaming in uncontrollable rivers down her cheeks. I feel like shit. She's filled with as much terror as I am. She's the one that lost him, after all. She sniffs quietly and wipes at her runny nose. I have the urge to go to her, wrap her in my arms like a mom would

104

do, but I'm not this child's mother. She might be Alex's child and maybe under different circumstances I could think of her as mine too, but right now as it stands, she's only a threat to my future.

"Babababa." I hear him before I see him. My heart lurches with hope.

"Laurent?" I whisper into the air.

I bend down to his level and push away the reeds that line the shore. Then I see him. He's playing in the shallow water among tall reeds. He's practically alligator bait splashing and giggling the way he is. I snatch him up and hold him close. "Oh, sweet, sweet baby, you scared us."

Once I reach the shore, Albertine hops up and down and claps her hands together. "You saved him! You saved him!" She squeals and then holds onto both of his legs and giggles, "His toes are blue! His lips too!"

I bend and set him on my knee, angling him in the moonlight so I can see better. "I don't think his lips are blue, it's just that the moonlight makes them look that way."

"No! They're blue!" She yells back at me.

I roll my eyes and then stand, ready to forget this even happened. "Come on, let's get back to that movie. Are you ready for popcorn?"

"I don't really want to watch the movie anymore." Boredom laces her words. "I want to talk to Daddy — I miss him."

Her words cling to the humid air and yet still send a chill through me. "Maybe we can call him before bed tonight."

"Okay. I'm going to tell him Laurent almost got eaten by alligators tonight."

"What? No — Albertine you can't." Terror lodges in my throat.

"Yes, I can." Albertine stops at the gate and glares up at me. "I tell my daddy everything."

CHAPTER TWENTY-TWO

Gravel bites into the pads of my feet as I run down Ocean Boulevard. Palm Beach's grandest estates flank one side of the street and the Atlantic Ocean roars in my ears from the other. Hot tears cram behind my eyelids as my knees tremble and wobble. I gasp when my freshly-painted toe catches the edge of a crack in the pavement and sends me stumbling. I catch myself just before face-planting into the concrete. I sob, swiping itchy wetness off my cheeks. I plant myself in a patch of rich green grass, hanging my head between my knees and letting the tears come freely now.

I shove the memory of the man I just left in the penthouse at The Breakers into the darkest recesses of my mind.

Hugo promised this would be an easy date. He said this is one of his most exclusive clients — made me swear that I'd cater to his every need because I am the only one he trusts to do this job. Hugo knew I didn't want to do any more dates — he knew I was trying to move on from this life — but the money was too good to pass up.

Never trust a man, my mother cackles in my head. I guess I had to learn this lesson the hard way . . . again.

Now here I sit, my ass in the grass wearing only a torn dress and hot tears. Now I know that a ten-thousand-dollar date is too good to be true. I thought I'd seen everything. I try to scrub the vicious look the man had when he lunged for my neck with both hands — I ducked and ran out of the penthouse without my heels, without my clutch, without my phone.

A series of sputtering clicks jerks me from my nightmare and then freezing cold water douses me.

"Fuck." I sob, standing as the sprinklers spin and whirl around me. "Fuck. Fuck. Fuck."

I grit my teeth, pulling the crisply folded hundred-dollar bill from the tiny pocket sewn into my bra. My emergency cash. In the five years I've been escorting, I've never had to use it. Until tonight. Fuck Hugo. If I had my phone I'd block his number right now. I continue my walk down Ocean Avenue. If only everyone in Pahokee could see me now; small-town girl makes it big . . . in the escort business. I force the sense of shame down deep and take in a lungful of salty ocean air. A fresh wave of calm comes over me as I walk. By the time I find the next main cross street and manage to flag down a cab, my feet are bleeding and it's nearly five a.m.

I prattle off the address to the cab driver and he huffs once when he realizes I need him to take me into Miami.

"Get me there as quickly as you can and there's an extra tip for you," I spit, annoyed that he can't see that I've had a rough night.

He grunts, then peels off from the curb in the direction of the expressway. I suck in a measured breath and let my eyes fall closed as we travel farther away from my past. The next time I open my eyes, sunshine is chasing away the shadows. The cab comes to a slow stop under the canopy of a palm-lined street. I look up to the familiar peaked roofline of the bungalow and can't help feeling soothed by the absolute wholesome quality of it. Lately I've been feeling like I don't fit into this life — but the last eight hours have changed my mind. I will do anything to avoid a repeat of last night. I will force myself to fit into this life even if it kills me.

"Thank you." I thrust the hundred-dollar bill over the front seat and then crawl out of the cab. I reach the front door and then realize I don't have my keys. I bend, lifting up the small garden frog that's perched on the porch step to find the spare key. I shove it in the lock and open the door as quietly as I can. Walking on my bare, bloody feet proves painful as I aim for the shower. A moment later I'm stripped out of my little

black dress and stepping into the hot water. New tears mingle with the old ones and the hot shower spray, both working to loosen my muscles but it does little to dislodge the pain that's settled on my heart. Time freezes as I stand there, gathering resolve to cultivate the future I want for myself — I've already laid the groundwork. I only have to seal the deal. And I'll need to seal the deal quickly — my bank account is going dry. Ten thousand dollars would have carried me for at least a few more months, but without it, I'll need to figure out something else. Something that does not include Hugo.

"Mornin' babe, how was the modeling gig?" His voice yanks me from my thoughts.

Alex.

"It was good," I plaster on a smile with my lie. I've learned you catch more flies with honey, even when it feels like a hornet's nest is swarming in my gut. There is power in softness. Like the passion in a kiss or the thunder with the rain, I need Alex to trust me if I have any chance at keeping him. And I need to keep him. I can't imagine a way forward without him. If I lose him, I'll be stuck with Hugo and all the men. I can't go there again. "How was your night?"

"Great — won some money on fantasy football and worked on an updated plan for the new atrium in City Hall." He's in a good mood this morning. If he only knew where I really was all night he'd have a different tone. Shame and guilt swim together in my system, threatening to take me under again.

"That's fun!" I do my best to match his cheer.

I finish washing my hair and body, then turn to find him waiting for me with a fresh towel. His smile is warm and inviting and despite the night I've had, I want nothing more than to fall into his arms right now. Never trust a man, my mother's voice rings again. But you can trust this one, I remind myself.

No words are exchanged as I step out of the damp shower and into his waiting arms. He wraps me in the towel, tucking it sweetly over my breasts before running his palms up and down my arms. He generates heat as he guides me into our bedroom. We pause by the window that overlooks the small fenced back yard. It teems with fuchsia bougainvillea trellis' and all types of palms. It's our little oasis in the heart of Miami, and even though my mind isn't mapped for things like peace and calm — chaos and upheaval are a more natural state for me — I need this. I need him.

"I wanted to wait for the perfect moment to do this," Alex spins me in his arms, "but right now feels right."

He locks his eyes with mine and then drops down to one knee. "Sugar," his grin tips playfully, "you are the most honest, kind, and loving woman I've ever met. If you'll have me, I'll dedicate my life to being the man that you deserve. Will you marry me?"

Waves of emotion nearly knock me out as I stare down at this man waiting for my answer. The more I know about life, the more I realize that I know nothing at all. But the one thing I know for sure? This man is good. Correction. This man is great. He may think he needs to spend his life striving to be the man I deserve, but the truth is that he has more class in his pinky finger than I could ever hope to have. I've never thought of myself as the marrying type — how could I possibly bring love, nurturing, and joy to someone's life when my own childhood was devoid of such things? But the love coming from this man's eyes has me held captive. He overflows with patience and empathy — characteristics so lacking in myself. Alex is the kind of man that was meant to raise children. I can't begin to think about what my life would be like if we hadn't met. I wouldn't have made it — life, my past — it would have taken me down.

Our gazes linger, something like love stirring in my soul for the first time.

I bend to his height. He curls me into his embrace. "I would love to marry you . . ."

CHAPTER TWENTY-THREE

Genevieve

"Do you hate me?"

Alexandre huffs in response, his hands tightening around the wheel of his BMW as we fly down the road. It's after midnight and despite all of my best efforts, I can't unplug the feeling that it's just better if I'm home right now. I'm also struggling to be around this man after finding lingerie tucked in his duffel bag. I haven't mentioned it to him because just the thought of it cracks my heart wide open. Anyway, maybe it's better to give him all the freedom he wants so when I file for divorce I'll have more than enough reason for doing so. If I can prove he's unpredictable and doesn't prioritize our children maybe I'll even get full custody of them.

"I just have this weird feeling—"

"I know all about your feelings, Gen." The edge in his voice is all the indication I need that he's irritated. Probably more than irritated, but he's always hidden his anger well. It's one of the things I used to love about him, but now I'm concerned he's just stuffing everything down until he explodes one day like a pressure cooker.

"Maybe we could go away for New Years — the other wives mentioned a ski getaway in Aspen — that sounds fun. I bet Albertine would love it."

Alex grunts once. "The partners already booked a golf getaway in Phoenix that week — didn't I tell you?"

"Oh." I sigh.

"Besides — I just tried to give you a getaway and here we are, cutting it short." I can hear the anger percolating in his voice. He fingers the tag on the small pink flamingo he purchased for Albertine at the gift shop at The Breakers earlier today. Before I ruined our romantic getaway.

"I'm sorry — there's just no way I could sleep being so far from Albertine . . ."

"Look — I'm sure the nanny is doing a great job, if there were any issues I'm sure she would have called."

"Would she though? Would she? Because I've really only known her a few weeks."

My husband sighs. "Well, you checked her references, right?" I don't dare share the fact that I *did not* in fact check her references, somehow it just . . . slipped my mind. "I thought the all-day private daycare for Albertine was supposed to make things easier on you, why does it seem like everything is worse?" he adds.

"It's not a daycare, it's an accredited, Montessori-certified school — the gold standard in early childhood education and development . . ." I trail off because I know he doesn't care, not really. "And everything is not worse." That statement feels like a lie even as I say it.

"Bullshit—" his grip tightens on the wheel and I can't help but get the sense that he'd rather it be my neck that he's wringing. His eyes narrow. He doesn't believe me. I can tell. "Why all the questions lately? Why are you always wondering where I am? Asking me about other women in the office and how much time I spend with them — feels like I'm under a damn microscope with you lately."

I gulp down my guilt because he's right. This is no way to live, walking on eggshells without a stitch of trust between us. When did the trust trickle out of our relationship? Was it one defining moment or a series of small nothings that added up to something over time? I wish not for the first time that I had a guide for this — a healthy marriage to look to when doubt creeps in.

"I keep trying to give you what you want, but I'm starting to think maybe I can't." He presses his lips together. "Hell, maybe you don't even want me to." Tension tightens his sharp jawline. The fine stubble that I used to love to run my fingers through now contains flecks of salt and pepper that make him look so handsome and distinguished; he fits the role of a Palm Beach husband perfectly. And here I am — numb, sad, dead inside. "Gen . . ." my husband's warm voice cuts through the silence in the car, "I'm afraid I'm losing you again."

His words sever my soul. I have never wanted to hurt this man, but what if keeping him is killing me? I can't help feeling this way — like we're slow dancing in a burning room and only one of us will make it out alive.

I turn my gaze down to my clasped hands. The giant, four-carat teardrop diamond Alexandre gave me for our engagement sparkles in the moonlight. I finally breathe, "I'm sorry."

Alexandre doesn't acknowledge my apology. Probably because he knows it's hollow. How can I apologize if I don't even know what exactly I'm apologizing for?

My husband flips on the blinker to turn into our neighborhood, the sharp *ding ding ding* feels like an ax splitting my skull.

We're home. For now.

CHAPTER TWENTY-FOUR

Adeline

"I'm going to check on Albertine." The deep timbre of Alex's voice echoes through the main level and jerks the baby awake in my arms.

"Ssh," I pat his back and he settles back to sleep instantly. I continue to rock the little boy in the dark and wait.

Within minutes I hear the loud clack of Gen's Louboutins through the kitchen. The baby makes a soft snoring noise and Gen spins, her eyes landing on mine. "Oh my God! You scared me!"

"Sorry, Ms. Did something happen during your getaway?"

"Oh, no. I just — we were worried about the children. I guess I don't feel comfortable leaving them overnight so soon."

I don't reply because the implication is clear. She doesn't trust me. I'm the last person she should trust so I guess her instincts are on point.

"Is the baby having trouble sleeping?" She settles on the lounger next to us.

"Who isn't?" I murmur. "It's the full moon, I think it makes everyone a little stir crazy."

"Does it?" Gen raises one perfectly Botoxed brow.

"I think so. Even Albertine was bouncing off the walls tonight — she wanted to call you before bed but I explained that parents need time to themselves sometimes too."

"Oh." Gen kicks off her heels. They clatter against the polished floor and Laurent jerks awake before falling right back asleep. Gen doesn't seem to notice that practically every move she makes is loud and distracting, she's like a selfish child herself, no wonder she's struggling to make someone else the center of her universe.

"Can I be honest with you, Adeline?" Gen's tone lowers an octave, as if she already hasn't been revealing every last thought that pops into her head when it comes to me.

"Of course, Ms."

"Please, I told you, call me Gen when it's just us."

It takes everything in me not to bark out a laugh. The pretentious perfectionism this woman exudes is enough to choke on. I will never call her Gen. She can think we're friends all she wants but that's one thing we will never be.

"Alexandre probably hates me. I can't even say I blame him. I think I hate myself most days."

"Don't be so hard on yourself — you're just doing the best you can in an impossible situation," I say.

"You think?" Her tone is soft, seeking, in need of understanding or validation.

"I know." I pat Laurent on the back as I rock him slowly. "The first five years of parenthood are a warzone — if it doesn't break you at least a few times you're not doing it right, trust me." I smile inwardly. Gen is too damaged to see through my concern, all she's looking for is a friend among the throngs of day-drinking mommy zombies.

"It does feel like I'm getting buried under all the responsibility a little more every day."

I nod as if I know exactly what she's talking about. In truth, I'm the one that will hammer the final nail in her coffin, but she won't know that until it's too late.

"It's nice to think it would be better if Alexandre was home all week helping, but the reality is he does little to help when he is here so why would I expect anything else? Men just don't have that same nurturing gene that moms have, ya know?"

"It's all on you, all the time. I get it." I validate her worst feelings. "Motherhood does feel like getting the short end of the stick a lot."

I glance around the beautiful, gilded cage she calls home. I'd spend the next two decades of my life raising these little hellions if it meant I wouldn't have to worry about a roof over my head and where my next meal was coming from.

Gen never called the previous employers listed on my business card and it's a good thing she didn't. I had a lie ready but it might have all blown up in my face if she'd tried. I'd told her the number for the Fountains was old when we met — a family that I've never even met much less worked for — and I listed my back-up cell number as one of the other references. If she'd called I would have done my best to disguise my voice but it would have been sketchy at best. Luckily, Gen is under the impression that I'm a good fit for her family, but it's only because I've made her believe it's so. If I'd told her the true story about my life — how I was born white trash — she'd never have invited me into her home to care for her precious family.

"I hired you to be a surrogate parent for my children, but who do I hire to be a surrogate husband for me?" Her chuckle is dark, sadness settling in the quiet between us.

"Men have a way of avoiding what they don't want to see," I say in a measured tone.

"Do they ever. I just wish I wasn't the thing he wanted to avoid," she admits. "Sometimes I wonder if this would be easier if I were doing it alone — the stress of missing him, of needing him when he's not here, of trying to explain why this isn't working for me like it is for him, is exhausting and triggering for my anxiety. He thinks I just need medication, a nanny, and some mommy friends to feel complete but he's forgetting that I need him too. I need him." She swipes the emotion pooling in her eyes. "I don't think he needs me though. He used to see me — *really* see me. He used to ask me questions — what makes me happy and what makes me sad — he went out of his way to *know* me, now I'm just like the help — nothing more than the mother of his children. I'm to be seen and not heard. And heck . . ." she laughs ruefully, "he doesn't even see me all week."

I nod empathetically.

"Everyone thinks that motherhood and marriage go hand in hand, but what if one breaks the other? What if what's required to give life is at the cost of another? Why does it feel like the day I gave birth I gained a new life and lost my identity in one push?"

I let her question hang heavy between us for long moments before I finally offer: "Sometimes couples float apart, Ms."

"Yeah?" She turns to me. "Maybe sometimes couples float so far apart that it feels impossible to get back to shore — like maybe we've both forgotten ourselves and what we were even swimming for." She's squirming, uncomfortable in her discomfort. "Sometimes I just feel nothing at all — not love, not hate, not anything. Do you think this is what the end feels like? Some couples can work through it, some can fight for one another, or do it for the children and the life they thought they wanted, but what if I have nothing left to give? What then?"

I don't respond because I'm sure she doesn't want me to. I'm not even sure if she realizes that I'm still here — witnessing her darkest thoughts in the middle of the night while her baby sleeps in my arms.

"I'm sorry—" she stands awkwardly, loops the straps of her heels in one finger and then glances at me. "I shouldn't say these things. Mothers shouldn't think this way. *Chin up and get through it, baby girl*, that's what my dad would say." She frowns as if she doesn't believe it herself. "Anyway, you're okay to put the little guy to bed, right? I'm exhausted, if I don't lay my head on a pillow soon, who knows what kind of nonsense I'll be spewing." She blinks, swallows, then casts her eyes around the room.

"Yes, Ms. I'll take care of him."

Gen nods, sadness still rimming her irises. "Thank you, Adeline."

"Anything you need, Ms."

Gen walks out of the living area and down the long hallway that leads to the staircase. She looks like a woman beaten down by life. I know I was hired to help her, but all I can focus on is ruining her. And she's making it so easy.

The end is imminent for them.

I rock the baby in my arms and hum as a slow smile splits my lips. He's so sweet, so innocent, so in need of a real mother's love. Albertine too — she's a hellraiser but only because she senses her mother is a million miles away even when they're in the same room.

I'll miss them when they're gone.

CHAPTER TWENTY-FIVE

Genevieve

"So, Genevieve," Marissa begins in her abnormally slow, unbearably manufactured cadence, "how is Alexandre handling being away from Palm Beach all week? I'd go absolutely *insane* spending every day downtown but maybe he likes it?"

"Oh," I sip my mimosa and avoid eye contact with the other wives, "he's liking it, I think."

Fawn raises an eyebrow. "Do you ever visit him in Miami during the week? I'd look for every excuse possible to put on a short little dress and go dancing." She sips as I suppress a cringe.

"No, he likes to focus. I'm so busy with the children all week anyway, I hardly have time to . . . well, you know . . . do *anything*." All the women nod at my admission. "I feel like I hardly talk to him anymore anyway," I say before I can stop myself. I never reveal what I'm really thinking to these women. I've learned that all those pearls and Chanel are meant to disguise mean girls. They're quick to gossip and even quicker to stab a friend in the back when it suits them.

"Jonathan and I have been seeing this phenomenal therapist for couples counseling — I can give you her number, it's been wonderful just having a designated time every week to sit and talk to each other without any distractions—" Fawn slow drawls in that perfect way she does and it makes my stomach coil and knot.

I stand, unable to take any more of their pity. "I think — I think I should go check on Albertine."

I rush back into the house, stand just inside the door jamb and then do my best to control the tears threatening to cover my face. I sob once, then take a deep breath and push the wetness away.

"She's losing it — you can see it in her eyes." Fawn's voice carries through the afternoon heat and lands on my ears. Their voices carry farther than they think, I can hear them clear as a bell from at least a few dozen yards away.

"Ssh," Marissa hisses. "Didn't I tell you something is off with her? I don't think she's handling being alone with the kids all week very well."

"Or maybe Alexandre is cheating on her," Fawn retorts.

Hannah, another one of the wives chimes in. "That's exactly why I'd never let my husband work away all week — men are only animals, all it takes is a short dress and a pair of heels and it triggers their hunting instinct. Believe me, if my husband worked away all week I'd know it's the beginning of the end for us."

"Please — this is all new for her. What would you do in her situation? It's practically impossible," Marissa says before I hear her voice lower a few octaves as she says something else I can't hear.

"That's why I offered my therapist—" Fawn twitters.

"Danielle said she saw her coming out of Katherine Connelly's office the other week," Hannah mentions the lawyer I visited, "if you ask me, I think the time for marriage counseling has passed. I think they're on the fast-track to divorce."

"If Genevieve ends up divorced and single parenting she'll have a breakdown for sure," Fawn chimes in. "Single motherhood just isn't meant for some moms, who knows what would happen."

"Mm," I hear the other two agree. I curse the day Adeline and I ran into Marissa at the market the other week. I find myself cursing basically every interaction with them, so why do I keep inviting them over for mimosas and brunch?

I turn to take in my reflection in the hall mirror. What about me makes them think I would have a breakdown if I had to single parent these children? Do they have some sort of maternal sixth sense that they find lacking in me? I take in the high cheekbones and sallow hollows of my cheeks. I look exhausted because I feel exhausted — my soft skin feels hardened and worn, the sparks in my eyes have turned dull and lifeless. I don't recognize myself. I fell from the top of the world and now I'm invisible. I guess I wasn't ready to be invisible yet — not when they were born, not now, maybe not ever.

I think of Laurent's all-nighters and how Albertine had terrible colic for the first year of her life. It felt then like she only cried when she was with me, like nothing I could do would ever be enough. Every tear felt like a betrayal. She was supposed to want me and I was supposed to want her, so why did it feel like we're both still barely tolerating each other? Is this as deep as our mother-daughter relationship will ever be?

A fresh wave of tears overwhelms me. "I just want more time for myself. I just want a break from them." I sob and push the itchy tear tracks away. "Why does it feel like finding myself again is too much to ask?"

CHAPTER TWENTY-SIX

Adeline

Gen sniffs softly, gathering herself in the hall before heading back to the mommy zombies by the pool. I understand why she feels like she doesn't belong.

She's not supposed to belong. No one is.

That's the ultimate game these women are playing. Some women wear perfectionism like a comforting blanket when it's nothing more than a sharply cultivated defense mechanism. If they can convince you that they're untouchable, they remain safe from the true grit of motherhood and marriage and life. It's hard to hurt the woman that appears to have everything, but just a scratch beneath the surface reveals a truckload of tranquilizers just to get them through the daily delusion.

Life is what we make of it and these women have lost their identities to motherhood. On some level I get it. Motherhood takes more than it gives. Sometimes it takes everything we have and more. And sometimes all that giving in the service of another human causes us to lose everything of ourselves. New sensible, mom haircuts. Lululemon workout gear all day. Louboutins and Louis bags at the PTA meetings. They make me want to puke too. All of them are trying so hard to be what's expected of them. But the more Gen tries to fit their mold, the closer she gets to breaking.

Right where I want her.

A flash of Alex's body pressed to mine comes back to me.

I blink away the memory. It's so intense I can taste his skin on my tongue. How funny a feeling it is to remember every inch of someone's body and soul and have them recall nothing of yours. I guess some small part of me had hoped my presence would trigger his memory, but maybe he's lost himself to this life too. Maybe the only way this man gets through his day is by putting one foot in front of the next, never stopping to wonder if this is still the life he wants.

From the playroom window I can see that Gen has rejoined her friends on the patio. She's explaining something to them and then within a moment they're all standing, finishing their mimosas, and lifting their giant designer totes onto their shoulders. I'm glad they're leaving — I don't need any more sets of eyes on me. Every extra pair that could identify me in a line-up or for a police sketch artist is a problem. My only goal, outside of dismantling this sacred union one block at a time, is to get in and out cleanly. I have regrets about meeting Alex in Miami last week — there are a thousand ways that could backfire on me — but how could I help myself? It'd been so long . . . when the opportunity to deliver the file fell into my lap the desire to see him was too strong to walk away from.

Just as the mommy zombies vacate the pool patio, the man of the house saunters through with Albertine in his arms. Seeing him be a dad has had an effect on me that I didn't anticipate. I never wanted children, was never willing to give everything of myself, but seeing the natural way he parents draws me to him more than ever before.

Is it so wrong to take Gen's life out from under her if she doesn't want it anyway?

I struggle to control the impulse to go to him. It will do me no good to insert myself into his life any more than I already have. *Slow and steady wins the race.* I recall another old saying from my father.

If I want to get this man back, it will take more than one appointment with a divorce attorney. I need to make sure this split is permanent.

CHAPTER TWENTY-SEVEN

Genevieve

"Adeline!" My voice bounces off the cathedral ceilings.

"Out here, Ms.!" Comes her faint voice.

I shove open the back door and call out to the pool, "have you seen the keys for the Audi?"

Adeline spins in the lounger, Laurent's chubby body in her lap as they watch Albertine swim.

"They should be in the dish by the garage door, Ms."

I groan, because obviously I already looked there. "Not there!"

Adeline's features remain stoic. It's something that unnerves me about her — her total unshakeability. I have never spent a moment feeling as cool, calm, and collected as she always looks. I have a drawerful of prescriptions that hardly touch my constant state of anguish and anxiety while she seems to have been born with this ever-present sense of peace. I can't stand it — the way she so effortlessly cares for my children, as natural as if they were her own.

"Hm . . . Are they hanging on the key rack in the kitchen?" Adeline calls back to me.

I sigh, already exhausted by this day.

I let the door swing closed behind me and head for the kitchen where I promptly find the keys to the Audi. I know I didn't leave them here because I never do, but Alexandre probably had to move my car in the garage to get to something so I don't think much of it. I toss the keys in my bag and then head down the hall. I find the Audi backed into place, also something I don't do, so this is just further confirmation that Alexandre must have used the Audi for something. I like that he took the time to back my car into the garage, he's always been thoughtful with the small gestures, less so with the big ones.

I punch the button to start the Audi and shift into drive, angling around the circular drive that rings the fountain. As the driveway straightens out I hit the button on my visor to open the iron swing gates. They move open slowly and I have to tap the brakes to slow down or I'll fly right through them. But something is wrong. Very, very wrong because when I tap the brakes, nothing happens.

My heart throttles my throat as I repeatedly push on the brakes. They're not working. The Audi doesn't slow down even a little bit. I scream and grip the wheel, searching for any direction I can angle the car to safely stop my momentum. I curse the magnolia trees that line the drive — such a striking feature in the realtor photos and now a death sentence. The gates are swinging wider on their slow track but at this point, even if they do open wide enough to let me through, that will only put me barreling into traffic.

"Stop, stop, stop, please." I cry, still pumping the pedals to no avail.

It's then I realize the row of azaleas that flank the last pair of magnolias might be enough to stop me without throwing me headfirst into the windshield. I angle the steering wheel in the direction of the bushes and then close my eyes tightly and pray.

And then, with a sickening thud, the Audi comes to a sudden stop lodged in the azalea bushes.

My head hurts, but I think it's a tension headache more than an injury. Or maybe I'll have whiplash for a month. I slide a palm over my face and then around my neck to rub away the ache. Why would the brakes go out all of a sudden? Wouldn't there have been a sign or symptom that they were in need of repair before this point? And didn't we just have it at the dealership last month for an all-point inspection?

And then it occurs to me: the missing keys and the Audi backed into the garage . . .

Someone did this intentionally.

CHAPTER TWENTY-EIGHT

Adeline

"I'm glad you're all here." I start, before Gen joins the group. As far as I know she's still sleeping, having forgotten the women were coming over. "Someone cut the brake lines on the Audi yesterday."

The mommy zombies gasp in unison.

"Did you call the police?"

"Who would do that?"

"Did you check the security cameras?"

"Maybe we should hire a security guard to watch the neighborhood."

I have to contain a chuckle at the way they all seem to be of the same hive mind.

"The security system hasn't been working — Alex called the company but they're booked out six weeks."

"What about the police? They should know," Marissa chastises.

I shake my head but don't reply.

"What if it happens to one of us?" she continues. "Maybe an officer should be patrolling this neighborhood regularly. Remember when the Morales' had that peeping tom at the end of the street?"

"I don't think that was a peeping tom, I think that was just the gardener she was having a little dangerous liaison with, if you know what I mean," Hannah quips then sips her sparkling water.

"Either way — they should know." Marissa is clearly worried. All of them look like they've just seen a ghost — clutching at their pearls as they try to imagine what kind of monster would want to target women *like them*.

"I'll call and file a report. I think this is something we should deal with ourselves though. I was thinking maybe a neighborhood watch? Or Hannah — your house is within eyesight of this one, maybe your security cameras caught something?"

"I'll have Derek check." She sips and smiles.

"It's just so rattling — feeling like we're being watched or targeted. I don't understand it. Who would do something so evil?"

The other women nod, worry lacing their irises.

"No one in this house has been able to sleep since it happened. Let me tell you, I felt real terror for the first time in my life when it happened."

"That sounds truly awful," Hannah clasps a hand over her heart.

"Things like these are never random — I've watched enough *Dateline* to know that. Is there anyone that might be upset with Alexandre maybe?" Marissa asks.

"How would they even get in? This is supposed to be the safest luxury community in Palm Beach — why do we have a guard shack at the front gates if no one is ever there?" I complain.

"Cutbacks — they replaced the guard with a digital security system."

"It wouldn't be hard to sneak in though — crawl through some azaleas and over the wall at the back of the community—"

"Or—" Marissa interrupts, "it's someone *inside.*"

"What do you mean?" Hannah stops sipping, eyes round with terror. "You think it's one of us?"

"It could be," Marissa confirms.

"But why?" Hannah squeaks.

"Why not?" Marissa shoots back.

"It's been such an exhausting few days around here," I murmur as if to myself.

"Oh, I can't imagine. I wouldn't sleep a wink if I thought a crazed lunatic was haunting my property at night while my family sleeps."

"*If* that's the case," I say.

"What do you mean?" Hannah leans closer.

"Well, that's the thing, Alex checked the brakes — *he* says no one cut them. He's worried the anxiety and sleeping meds—" I halt mid-sentence, as if I've just revealed too much. I need these women to know that Gen can't be trusted; that she's neglectful and irresponsible and not fit to raise these children.

"Meds?" Marissa raises one perfect brow.

"I don't really want to repeat what he said . . ." I utter, as if embarrassed.

"Please. Honey, now isn't the time to be secretive—" Juanita whispers.

"I wouldn't bring it up if I didn't think something about it was strange — he's worried it's starting to affect the kids but . . ." I look around the table of riveted women, "It's just been such a hectic season in this house. Albertine has been acting out and no one here is sleeping through the night, so when something like this happens . . . Some of the anxiety medications in that bathroom are enough to knock out an elephant and maybe they add to the confusion and maybe even cause paranoia. Add a mixed cocktail or two and who knows what might happen, right?" I let my words trail off as Albertine runs across the patio at us.

The women look around at each other as if they've just been told the Palm Beach secret of the century.

"I'm going swimming before lunch!" Albertine squeals as she runs by.

"That sounds fun, baby," I say. "Why don't you show us your backstroke?"

Albertine nods, then jumps into the pool.

I blink back a vision of her lifeless body floating peacefully and plaster a cheery smile on my face. After all, I have a role to play, just like Gen does.

Only I'm a better actor than she is.

CHAPTER TWENTY-NINE

Genevieve

Sunshine wraps me in a warm blanket as I watch the children play at the beach that's walking distance from our house. Laurent is sliding his chubby little hands in the winter-white sand as Albertine dodges the whitecaps that roll onto shore. She bends to inspect the tiny white shells that are left in the wake of the waves, picking out the most interesting ones to show Laurent. He coos softly, pointing to them in her open palm before picking one up and putting it in his mouth.

"Laurent! No, no!" Albertine sweeps the tiny shell from his mouth before I can even peel myself off of the beach towel. She's such a good little mother — she has a natural instinct for it, I can tell, mostly because it was an instinct I wasn't born with. I have scrounged and scraped for every ounce of maternal feeling in me and it still doesn't feel like enough. Can she feel that we are not connected as a mother and daughter should be?

It's easier with Laurent. He's a baby. He's a *boy*. But with her . . . I feel incensed about everything. It's as if her entire existence is meant to remind me that I'm not good enough.

That I am broken and lacking and not worthy of being her mother and she can see through my carefully constructed veneer. My own mother found fulfillment between the sheets with an ever-revolving door of men. Motherhood wasn't her superpower, catching wealthy men to abuse her and her children was. I've spent so much time outrunning what felt like my inevitable destiny, chasing perfection and forever failing, I can't help but feel like a hamster on a wheel. When Albertine's black Mary Jane shoes have a scuff, I have to control my anger. When her school uniform is wrinkled, I think of the judgment that will descend like clouds in the eyes of the other mothers. Some days I think this job is killing me, and then there are days like today — when everything just feels right.

Albertine is behaving, Laurent isn't crying, and my head isn't screaming with the need to escape.

Most of the days of the week I'm barely holding my head above water.

A vicious memory presses at my skull, demanding to see the light of day after so many years buried.

The swirling cloud of cigarette smoke that always envelops my mother. Tremors of seething violence as she overpowers me. Her face, as red as her cherry-stained lips as she spits her words of hate, perfectly-arched eyebrows knit together with contempt.

My mother, the only person I've ever met that can bring feelings of love and hate to the surface in the same moment. My father called her complicated. When I was eight, I called her mean. By the time I turned twelve, I knew she was so addicted to her pain, she'd never let it go — not even for me. Her only child. Cement hardens in my throat as I think about the woman that raised me — or *tried*. In truth, she wasn't fit to mother herself much less anyone else.

At my tenth birthday party she raged because the three-tiered carrot cake didn't have enough carrot. When I was twelve I pulled a steak knife on her after she spent an hour banging on my door in the middle of the night. She'd received an email from my science teacher earlier that day that she still couldn't get over — it was the first time she put her hands around my neck. It was also the last.

That day, blinking back exhausted tears, I told my science teacher that my mom had kept me up all night fighting. That she'd tried to choke me. That it hadn't been the first time she'd raged about the failure I was destined to become while keeping me up all night as she spun her violent chaos.

In the weeks that followed, I refused to speak to her — because if I didn't acknowledge her presence, how could I get into trouble? I dodged all of her verbal bullets for two weeks. Cleaning obsessively, always perfecting, but still never good enough to keep her abuse at bay. My childhood was spent in this way, forever expending effort to manifest my worth.

My plan to be neither seen or heard had a fatal flaw though. I underestimated her hatred for me. I realized how dark she was willing to go when she announced that she would be handing me over to the state — I would be raised in the foster care system. *"Let them handle you,"* she'd said. I refused to eat for days as I quaked with fear in my bed and she laughed. Mocked me for being a baby — how if I'd only listened to her she wouldn't have to do these things. And when the day arrived for the judge to hear her case — she walked me in front of the judge and, with manufactured tears in her eyes, promised to give me one more chance if I could only promise to behave. The judge dismissed the case and my mother left with a triumphant smile, her noose of control tightening a few more notches around my neck, but this time, her manipulations had new psychological flair. She proved then that this wasn't just between her and me — she had the system on her side. But karma knocked on our door hours later in the form of Child Protective Services. I was removed from my mother's house that night — my science teacher had asked for a well-check all those weeks ago and the department had only just gotten around to it. I smiled as they walked me out with a single suitcase of my things. I had no idea where I would next call home, but anywhere would be better than with her, I'd thought. But I couldn't have been more wrong. They sent me to live with my dad, exchanging verbal abuse for physical. I barely survived the people that raised me, suicidal thoughts haunting the edges of my mind from the time I was old enough to know what it meant to permanently opt out of this life.

I wanted to be a good mom. I wanted to be the mom I never had. I tried to be responsible and show up for Albertine in the ways my mother hadn't for me. I made healthy, organic meals and a reliable routine the focus of our lives. Clean clothes, countless activities, play dates and plenty of quality time. I gave Albertine everything I wanted for myself in a mother. But Albertine didn't want what I had to offer.

"Afternoon, Ms." Adeline appears from over my shoulder, pulling me from the past and back to the children playing in the gentle waves lapping the shore.

"Oh!" I press an open palm over my heart. "You scared me."

"I'm sorry. Laurent is out of oat milk—"

"Oh — I can't bring myself to move right now, the sunshine makes me so sleepy," I say, happy and sun-drunk. "Would you mind running up to the market? Oh, and while you're there can you stop by the pharmacy and see if Albertine's inhaler is ready? This prescription shortage is giving me so much anxiety — what if her allergies — ugh, I can't even think about it. Anyway, take the Audi, you know where the keys are."

"Sure, Ms.," Adeline replies. "Is there anything else?"

"No, I don't think so. Thank you, Adeline, you're such a lifesaver."

Adeline hums, turns to leave and then glances to the children. "Do you want me to take the kids, Ms.? The baby will probably be ready for his nap soon and I know he loves the motion of the car. It'll just take me a moment to walk him back to the house."

"No, no, it's fine. I'll be ready to go in soon anyway. I promised Albertine avocado toast for lunch — and I made her promise to help me make it." I trail off, sighing as I realize I'm going to have to *teach* her to make it, calling on patience I don't really have even on my best days.

"Okay, Ms." Adeline moves off slowly and I can't help but feel she's hovering for a reason — babysitting me as if she doesn't trust me. "I'll be back in a few."

"Bye, Adeline," I call into the warm breeze.

I swirl the bubbly glass of champagne in one hand before tipping it to my lips and emptying the glass. The fizzy bubbles heat my veins as my muscles relax a little deeper into the lounger. I smile softly, watching my babies play as the sunshine melts away the tension I've been feeling these last few days. I smile as I realize the older the kids get the more independence I'll have — that this baby phase is just that — a phase. And I can get through anything, right?

I yawn, stretch, then tip my sun hat over my eyes and let them fall shut for just a moment. My heartbeat slows and warmth curls through my body and unlocks the anxiety that's made me feel so tightly wound; so locked in a prison of my own making.

"Maman!" I wake with a jump. "Maman!"

"Albertine?" I call back, pushing the sunhat off my face. I blink away the blinding sunshine. Everything feels like a dream, sun flares blind my vision as the reflection of the water glistens and sparkles.

"Mommmmmy!"

"What?!" I hold a hand over my eyes to shield the sun as I search the shoreline for Albertine.

"Mommy! Mommy! Mommy!" Albertine shrieks again. "Look at Laurent! He's hiding!"

I jump off the lounger then as the reality of this moment slices through the haze of my mind. I run to the shore, eyes scanning for my baby. I see Albertine, but Laurent has just . . . *vanished.*

"Look, Mommy!" She points and giggles. "Laurent is sleeping!"

My eyes fall to the sandcastle where I see Laurent's chubby little fingers poking through the sand.

She buried him alive.

CHAPTER THIRTY

Adeline

"Laurent?" All I see is sand and waves and chaos as Albertine dances and giggles wildly around Gen, who is hunched over near the shore sobbing. "What's wrong?"

"She buried him!" Gen screams.

What the hell is she talking about? I've hardly been gone for forty-five minutes, what could possibly have happened?

I come around her shoulder and can see clearly for the first time what she means. She's rocking Laurent in her arms, tears streaming down her cheeks as she tries to brush sand away from his lips. He's awake, his eyes watery as if he's been crying but his cheeks are a shade of tomato and he seems . . . sluggish. Something isn't right. It's like he's been drugged or . . .

"Has he been in the sun since I've been gone?!" I reach for the baby but she turns away, clutching him tightly to her body.

"Where were you?!" Comes her vicious accusation.

"I went to the market — the oat milk — the inhaler—"

"Why didn't you tell me you were leaving?"

"I . . . I did," I whisper, shocked that she doesn't remember. It's almost like she wasn't even there for our conversation just an hour ago. "Ms. — I think he has sunstroke."

"It was Albertine — I–I don't know what happened." Gen's eyes are crazed as she holds his almost lifeless form to her chest.

"I think he needs a hospital, something is very wrong—"

"No, I–I think he'll be fine. He just needs a bath. He had sand in his mouth and, oh God, Albertine, why?" Fresh tears cover Gen's cheeks.

Albertine splashes in the waves as she watches us intently. Even she looks worried. She tosses a handful of tiny white shells at us and then yells, "Daddy will be so mad."

"Oh Albertine, shut up," I hiss and then catch myself and glance at Gen. She doesn't seem to have heard me, she's so caught up in her own grief. This woman is useless in the best of times and downright awful in the worst of them. I regret not following my gut instinct and taking the kids with me to the market. How absurd that I assumed that this woman was competent enough to watch her own children for an hour.

"He needs help." I crouch to her level and place a hand on the baby. He's burning up. "We need to call an ambulance."

"No — no, I don't need the neighbors to know anything about this," Gen spits.

"Gen." Anger laces my irises. "He's going to die."

"No — he's fine." She holds him away from her body. He doesn't move, his eyes heavy and unfocused.

Rage bunches my muscles and before I can think twice I snatch the little boy from her arms and run as fast as I can to the house. Gen and Albertine are shouting behind me, but they can't keep up — Albertine's legs are too small to carry her far quickly and Gen's system is soaked in sunshine and liquor. I run up the sandy pathway that leads to the gated community and almost slip when my feet hit the pavement. Gen and Alex's house is in sight now and my brain is working overtime trying to decide what to do when I get there. I run the last fifty yards to the house, pushing through the front doors and running straight for the main floor bathroom. I turn on the bathtub faucet to a cool temperature and strip him of his swim shorts and diaper. I use a washcloth to dab cool water on his body; under his neck and under his arms.

I need to call for an ambulance but I don't have enough hands to do everything. Gen and Albertine come clamoring down the hall then.

"Call the police. He needs help—"

"No. He's fine. Look — he's moving and his eyes look normal again. He just needs a nap and some Gatorade."

"Ms.—" I try to interrupt but she's not having it.

"Adeline! He's fine. Please, stop. I'm his mother." She drops to her knees on the floor and reaches for the little guy. As soon as she touches him he wails so loudly she backs away instantly.

"He's sunburned everywhere," I explain.

She cries softly before Albertine peeks over her shoulder to ask how her brother is doing.

"Please, take Albertine — we'll be fine. I'll make sure he's fine." I reassure her. Laurent is moving around a little more now but his skin is still a bright, unnatural shade of pink. I soak a towel in cool water and then wrap him in my arms and walk him into the kitchen in search of my phone. I dial emergency services and explain what's happened. The operator tells me an ambulance should arrive within four minutes.

I hang up the phone and listen quietly. Gen's sobs come from somewhere in the house and I can hear Albertine singing to herself upstairs, probably in her playroom.

I'm waiting patiently at the door when emergency responders arrive. I spend the next twenty minutes hovering as paramedics stick IVs in his tiny arms to hydrate him and cover him in cool medicated bandages. They confirm the little guy has been sun-poisoned and is severely dehydrated. When they ask what happened I explain that he spent a little too much time on the beach this afternoon. They give me a warning as if I am his mother, and then instruct me to give him children's Tylenol every 8-12 hours to keep the pain from his sunburns at bay.

By the time they're backing out of the circular drive, I know what I have to do.

Something has to give. We can't keep going on like this.

Just as I turn around to make Laurent a bottle with Gatorade, Gen appears, eyes bloodshot as they bounce from me to the baby in my arms. "We need to talk."

"Okay . . ." I say, hesitant about what might be coming.

"I don't know how this happened," she states.

I pause, because what does she want me to say? I know exactly how this happened. She got drunk and fell asleep on the beach and now here we are.

"I have a lot of concerns about your position with us going forward. If I can't trust you . . ." her tone is measured and haughty. She's more in control of herself than I've ever seen her — ironic how she's trying to peg me for this when I've just saved her son's life. "How could you have overlooked this?"

I swallow the fear that's crawled into my throat. "Overlooked what?"

"You should have told me you were leaving — I assumed you were watching the children." Her tone is dead serious.

"I did — Ms., you asked me to pick up your prescriptions." I try to defend myself.

"I did? Then where are they?"

"Where are what?" I ask, frustration and fear swirling like fog in my mind.

"The prescriptions," she spits, as if proving that I'm lying.

"They were — I asked the pharmacist but—"

"Right." She cuts me off. "I just can't believe this. I thought you were such a good fit — Alexandre isn't going to be happy." She glances down at the baby who is now fading off to sleep in my arms. "Can you put him down for his nap? I'm going to have to talk to my husband and consider what's to be done about this."

"What's to be done?" The words are barely audible as they leave my lips.

"We might have to terminate your employment. You understand, of course."

I don't argue. There isn't anything else I can say. Having a conversation with this woman is as good as talking to a brick wall — or worse — a zombie. A very dangerous zombie that's in charge of two precious babies. How could Alex leave the safety of his children up to this woman?

Gen turns, chin held in the air as she pulls a new bottle of champagne from the fridge and then walks off down the hall in the direction of the pool. I finish fixing Laurent's bottle of Gatorade and then bring him up to the nursery and settle myself in the rocking chair with him in my lap. He curls into the nook of my elbow like he belongs there and holds the bottle up and nurses from it greedily.

Then, I take out my phone and start a new email.

Dear Alex,
    I have become deeply concerned for the safety of this family . . .

CHAPTER THIRTY-ONE

Genevieve

Liar. Liar. *Liar.*

That's all I keep thinking as Adeline's excuses play on repeat in my mind.

I swirl my champagne flute as clouds of bath bubbles float and bob around me.

I did tell you. I did tell you. The prescriptions. I did tell you.

I didn't forget Adeline's words because she didn't say them. There was no conversation — at least not that I heard. I remember Adeline coming to check on me and the children while we were at the beach, but I thought she was staying. I didn't hear her say she was leaving. I didn't hear her mention the market or the prescriptions and I was *right* there, if she'd said it, I'd have heard it.

I think of Adeline standing in the doorway with my son in her arms as emergency responders arrived.

I know what she's doing.

She's trying to be the better version of me — trying to prove that *she* is a better fit for this family than I am. I'm watching this woman try to replace me and she's been working right under my nose this entire time. I think of Alexandre's anger at me for cutting our weekend getaway short, but maybe now he'll understand why — I just have to find a way to prove it or he'll accuse me of making more assumptions and accusations. I think of how attached Albertine is to this woman — how she's effortlessly inserted herself into my children's lives in just the two months she's been here. Already it seems that if I went away and never came back, I would not be missed.

Alexandre was right — I should have been wary of hiring strangers off the street. But something had to give. I was drowning without him here. I was so desperate for help and she fell into my lap like she was heaven-sent. A new au pair felt like an opportunity — like my prayers had finally been answered. Now I realize maybe it was the beginning of the end: the end of me, us, our family, everything. Hiring her is causing a further divide that could hasten our split, not delay or even prevent it like I'd hoped. A chill climbs up my spine. How could I have been so very wrong about this woman?

Adeline would be a better wife, mother, lover, even better at school pickup than me. If Alexandre knew what was best for his children he *would* replace me. The children deserve a mom like Adeline, not me — a crazy, emotional, worthless barely-holding-it-together mom. The truth is, I've been trying to convince myself not to run out on all of them since the day we brought Albertine home. From that moment, I was never the same. The baby books warned me that motherhood changes a woman, hormones and anxiety can fluctuate wildly in the first few months but it's been years and repressed fears still bubble to the surface on the daily.

Fears that I can't get a hold of. Fears that are threatening to break me.

I've been worried that Adeline and Alexandre will run away together, but maybe I've been worrying in all the wrong ways. Maybe I'm the one to be worried about.

142

CHAPTER THIRTY-TWO

Adeline

I'm thinking of ending things.

Starts Alex's email.

I find his message sitting in my inbox the next morning. I can't believe he's replied — I was lucky to find his work email in a pile of paperwork on his desk; when I sent the email yesterday about my concern for the safety of the family, I assumed the chances were good that it'd get stuck in his spam folder.

I continue to read:

Things haven't been the same since the babies were born. I wonder where the woman I once knew has gone. How did her love for me harden to resentment so quickly? I have regrets, who doesn't, but I can only repair our relationship if both people are on the same page — hell, it doesn't even feel like we're in the same book anymore. I've done my best to navigate this but I'm done. I promise you, this will break us.

My breathing is coming out shallow as I finish his email. This is not what I expected, but then, what did I expect when I practically insinuated that his wife is neglectful and downright dangerous with the kids? I don't know what to reply, maybe nothing. I type out a few sentences about being a support system, but that doesn't seem right — and I don't feel that way, not really. When I took this job I wasn't looking for a built-in family to care for, I was looking for Alex. Once I found out his precious daughter was enrolled at a private Montessori school in Palm Beach, I only went for a visit. I didn't anticipate running into *her* — his wife. And once I did, well, it felt like a path was set in motion that quickly spiraled out of my control. Now, here I sit, worrying over the safety of Alex's children as I try to drive a wedge between the man I still love and his wife.

Then it occurs to me what I should reply.

Maybe it's time to hire an attorney.

I hit send then tuck my phone into my bag just as a sea of kids descend on the parking lot. I spot Albertine through the throngs of people looking for her mother.

She's not here kid and she may never be again, I think to myself as I climb out of the Audi.

Albertine spots me and comes running across the school yard and wraps her tiny arms around my waist.

"Hey, Baby — how was school today?"

"It was great!" She's bouncing and joyous — so different from the sassy little girl that I met two months ago. Maybe my presence here really is calming for her, it's undeniable that she's grown more attached to me over the weeks than her own mother. I don't blame her though — cuddling with a drunk isn't fun — I still remember the smell of booze on my father's breath when he kissed me goodnight as a kid, and it still makes me cringe.

"Whaddya say we have dinner and watch a movie by the pool tonight? Does that sound fun?"

"That sounds like the best!"

I place a palm on her thin shoulder as we walk back to the car. "Great. Maybe you can even help me make dinner."

She nods. "Can we have mac and cheese again, Mommy?"

Her last word takes my breath away. "Honey . . ." I bite back tears because Albertine and I have grown so close, some days maybe I'm actually starting to wish I was her mommy too. "I love you so much but I think it's better if you just call me Ms. Ade—" I halt mid-sentence as the little girl's dark eyes brim with tears, "never mind. Call me whatever you want, baby."

Albertine wipes at her eyes as I open the back door of the Audi and she climbs into her car seat.

"Can we have ice cream after dinner tonight, too?" She hiccups softly.

"Ice cream *and* popcorn with a movie, huh?" I smile, tucking a blonde curl behind her ear as I buckle her in safely. "That sounds perfect."

The house is silent when Albertine and I walk into the kitchen twenty minutes later. She hooks her backpack on the hook in the mudroom just like she always does, then singsongs her way to the fridge before pulling out an apple. She swipes her stuffed puppy dog from the barstool and cuddles him close before wandering out to the pool. I watch her move on light steps, thinking what a sweet girl she is without her micro-managing mother helicoptering over her all the time. I pause at the doors that lead to the pool, watching Albertine dip her toes in the pool as she chatters away to Puppy. So sweet and innocent, so unaware of the storm brewing just beneath the surface of her family.

I hear the guest shower turn on and without thinking move down the hallway in the direction of the sound of the water. I know it's not Gen, because she's been resting all afternoon in her bedroom claiming she has a migraine. I find the door to the bathroom is cracked and I pause, letting my eyes focus through the haze of shower steam. I inch closer, trying to stay in the shadows when a draft clears the steam and Alex's naked form is revealed to me.

My heart catches in my throat.

Desire burns to life inside of me. The fire he lit half a decade ago still sizzles and smolders, just waiting to ignite again. Alex hums softly as he showers, turning as he soaps his body. The powerful muscles of his behind flex as he twists, arms reaching behind his head as he stretches in the hot spray of water. He's a work of art and I think for the first time he must spend at least some of his time in the city all week at the company gym. There is so much we still don't know about each other, I'm eager to rekindle what we had and learn even more about him.

Alex does a one-eighty in the shower spray, his gaze sliding across the room when he does. He blinks once, and when his eyes are open again I find them leveled with mine. My breath catches as I realize I've been caught. I'm standing here, practically acting like his stalker while I watch him in his most intimate of moments. I squeeze my eyelids together tightly as embarrassment heats my veins. When I open my eyes again, he's still looking. My lungs feel starved of oxygen as my heart thunders wildly. Why is he still looking at me? Is he angry? Turned on? Both?

I open my mouth as if to say something, but I'm not sure what. *I'm sorry,* maybe? What's the appropriate thing to say when you catch your employer in the shower?

His eyes narrow, brows knitting together a moment before he licks his lips with slow precision. The subtle gesture feels embedded with sexuality, the sensual way he moves is intoxicating. He slides a palm over his face and through his short hair, eyes closed, as if he's resigned to the fact that I am a prisoner to him. I am hooked, addicted as acutely as my own mother was to the parade of men she welcomed into her bed. I am no different than her, despite my best efforts to run from everything I thought she represented. And in running away, I ran right in a circle back to where I started.

Desperate for a man to need me so he'll never leave me.

CHAPTER THIRTY-THREE

Genevieve

Alexandre's gentle snores carry down the hallway as I move on soft steps into his office. I have to know what he's been up to all week in Miami. I don't want to believe that he could do this to our family, but after finding the skimpy lingerie in his bag, I don't know what else I'm supposed to believe. Now, according to my lawyer, I just need to find actual concrete evidence that proves that he's been spending time with someone else. Emails. Receipts. Flights. Anything.

My first stop is his laptop. I don't imagine I'll find anything good here — Alexandre is smart, he would never leave a trail, but I have to start somewhere.

First, I find his email inboxes. I sift through the last few weeks of emails in his personal account, it's mostly just spam and notifications about automatic bill payments, so I move on. The next is an old work account that has dozens of emails containing pdfs of blueprints and other work-related things. The next account is one we share together and is more automated emails from our bank, the neighborhood HOA committee, Albertine's school, and more. I move onto the next account and find it's another personal one that looks like it hasn't been used much. I scroll back a few weeks and then my blood runs cold.

A purchase confirmation for a flight to Fiji stares back at me.

I open the email and then gasp when I find that Alexandre booked two seats to Fiji for the week of New Years. The very week I asked for a family vacation to Aspen with the other wives. His story about his boss booking a trip to Phoenix for a last-minute work trip suddenly evaporates. He lied. He already has plans . . . with someone else. I bite back tears as I think about all we've been through these last few months — how I've been begging him for a family getaway or *anything*. If there's another explanation for this trip to Fiji, I can't imagine what it is.

My blood begins to boil as I hit print on the tickets. Two pages spit out of the printer on the side table and I fold them neatly and then tuck them in my pocket. I also snap a photo of the screen with my phone figuring I'll need to send this to my attorney as further evidence of my husband's dishonesty. I don't know if it's enough, but it's a start.

I move onto the next inbox and find that this is a new work email provided to him by the firm. All of the corre-spondence is between other partners, assistants, and clients. All except for one.

One message stands out to me because it's from Adeline.

My fingers shake as I open the message. I struggle to focus my eyes as rage colors everything a violent shade of red.

Dear Alex, I have become deeply concerned for the safety of this family . . . reads the first line. She calls him Alex, not Alexandre. My stomach coils and my vision blurs as I attempt to read the rest but it's hard — my eyes are greedy for my husband's reply. And when I scroll I find that there have been *many* replies. Alexandre and Adeline seem to have been conversing multiple times a day for over a week. She's been keeping tabs on me for him, reporting on the children, sharing school stories and projects . . . everything a mother would do. Everything I have been neglecting. Is that what he wanted? Regular check-ins about life here with us in Palm Beach? He wants to know that Albertine had avocado toast and eggs for lunch and swam after dinner? My heart cracks wide open because by the time I reach the bottom of the string of messages — the ones that have come in just the last twenty-four hours, I find that they have developed . . . *something*. A certain intimacy and trust has knit them together in their effort to protect the children from . . . *me*.

How could they do this? How could they betray me right under my nose?

It's me that pays her — not Alexandre.

It's me that hired her.

It's me that gave her this opportunity at a new life.

So why is it me that's become the outsider in their sick little love triangle?

My heart crushes like it's in a vice when I find the last two messages. His begins: *I'm thinking of ending things . . .* and her reply is simply: *Maybe it's time to hire an attorney.*

Anger pulses through my bloodstream as I realize it must be *her* lingerie that Alexandre had in his bag. She must have left it in Miami and he was bringing it home for her.

Here. To *my* home.

And it must be her he's taking to Fiji. I imagine tiny bikinis and colorful cocktails on a tropical beach as they chuckle about how smart they were, stealing my life right out from under me.

Let them think they've won now, but I'll have the last laugh. I always do.

I hit print on the string of emails and the printer immediately begins to spit out more than a dozen pages of their correspondence. I close Alexandre's email client and then shut the laptop.

I have all the proof I need now.

I gather the printed emails in my hands and exit Alexandre's office and head directly up to my bedroom. As the house silently sleeps, I begin to weave my web. I will catch them both, ensnare them like helpless flies and then suck the life out of them with slow, torturous pleasure.

I sneer, realizing my dear husband must have a savior complex if he's willing to fuck the help. I take the iPad from my nightstand and begin an email — a letter that will signal the end of this.

> *My dearest Alexandre,*
>   *I've recently stumbled into some startling news about the new au pair, Adeline.*

I bite down on my bottom lip as I consider how best to reveal my concerns without sounding like an accusing wife.

> *She is not who she claims to be. I've tried to get in touch with her previous employers but there are none. You were right — I was wrong to hire a stranger off the street.*

There. I think about the small business card she gave me in the parking lot the day we met. She admitted that the first number was out-of-service since the family had just moved. I never did try the others, I don't even know where that card is anymore. I hate sounding incompetent, but maybe if I can distract Alexandre with Adeline's inconsistencies and accusations he won't linger on my failings.

> *After learning about her startling history and questionable employment references, I'm concerned for the safety of our family. I'm concerned for myself. I think she's trying to hurt me.*

I reread my last sentence. Then I consider deleting it. I'm walking a fine line between cautious concern and outright paranoia. I don't need Alexandre to think it's me that's the problem — especially if they're already deep into an affair. I highlight my cursor on the last sentence and delete it. Laying on my concern too thick will only raise more concerns. Instead, I need to play ruthless. I'm not asking for my husband's permission to fire this woman, I'm telling him I am — his thoughts be damned.

> *I'm considering pressing charges on her for trespassing, false identification, fraud, and impersonation. I may even call Child Protective Services to let them know there's a woman running around Palm Beach impersonating a caregiver and moving into people's homes.*

I think about that day at the beach when Laurent swallowed sand and got sun-poisoned and Adeline called paramedics. Was it necessary? I don't think so, Laurent would have been just fine with a cool bath and Pedialyte. But the damage is done and I can't have another record so soon of anything strange occurring at our home relating to the children. Too many alarm bells will be triggered and I can't have that on top of everything else.

> *I plan to terminate her immediately, but I wanted you to know why first. I will begin my search for a new au pair. I'm sorry I didn't listen to you in the beginning.*

I add that last part to appease him. Do I actually feel a sense of remorse for not listening to Alexandre sooner? Not at all. But I've learned that sometimes you have to sacrifice being right to get what you want in the long run. Like throwing my husband a bone, I fluff his ego a little, reminding him that I am still the sweet, simpering wife he married.

A smug smile turns up my lips.

xoxo Yours

There. That will teach him to fuck the help.

CHAPTER THIRTY-FOUR

Adeline

"Goodnight, sweet girl." I peck Albertine on the cheek. She wraps her arms around me in a tight hug. It takes me by surprise at first. I give her a squeeze back and then tuck her down duvet around her form. "Snug as a bug in a rug."

Albertine giggles and then wipes at her sleepy eyes. "Goodnight."

I leave her room, shooting her one last smile before I hit the switch and the room is drenched in darkness. It's past Albertine's bedtime, but it's only Saturday night, so I figure it's not the end of the world. She spent most of the afternoon playing in the pool with her dad before they made dinner together and then played board games on the back patio while her favorite movie played on the projector screen. It was a great day — but Gen was nowhere to be seen. She spent all day in her bedroom and when I tapped on the door to ask if she needed anything, a grunt was the only reply. I figured that meant she was taking some time to herself — not that that would be different from any other day, but I digress.

I make my way down the spiraling staircase, moving on soft steps so I don't disturb Gen sleeping. When I reach the main floor I find that Alex is still out on the patio. I linger, watching him as he relaxes. He's as beautiful and reticent as he ever was — it's funny, the things that draw us to people are the very things that get under our skin with time. My eyes drop to the side table where Gen usually keeps the keys to her Audi in a small porcelain dish. Instead of the keys though, I find an envelope addressed to Alex in Gen's tight handwriting.

I lift it from the dish and flip it in my palm to find that it's still sealed. Curiosity hums to life inside of me as I tuck the envelope deep into the pocket of my pants before turning back to the pool patio. Alex looks so relaxed, I hate to disturb him on my walk to the pool house, but I have no choice. I open the door, eyes trained on his profile. Approaching quietly, I admire the way the soft glow of the café lights shadow the angles of his face — the dark stubble that shades his jawline looks even more angular in the soft lighting. Moonlight glistens off the pool water as he sits cross-legged in a lounger looking up at the stars.

I consider trying to avoid him on my walk to the pool house, but I can't. All of my instincts are telling me to go to him.

"Can I get you anything?" I purr once I'm near enough. He turns, movements slow and measured as he takes me in. When our eyes lock, my stomach drops.

His dark irises spark to life before he pats the lounger next to him. "Join me."

I smile, moving around the lounger to settle at his other side. As soon as I'm comfortable he pulls my lounger up close to his. "Evening."

"Hi," I reply, hoping the moonlight hides the crimson that's climbed up my cheeks under his hot gaze.

"Is Albertine in bed?" The deep rumble in his voice shoots straight to my core.

"Yes. Snug as a bug."

He chuckles. "I love when you say that." His grin tips sideways and my stomach cartwheels. "We're lucky to have you — *all* of us."

An unexpected wave of emotion washes over me then. I don't know how to reply so I turn my gaze up to the starry sky and take a few deep breaths. There is a natural intimacy that still exists between us — as if no time at all has passed even though it's been years since we've been like *this*.

"You've been a rock these last few weeks—" he continues, "I should have taken time off to help—"

"Please—" I interject.

"No, it's—"

"Really, Alex." I turn my gaze back to the sky. "It's such a perfect night, I don't want to ruin it by talking."

He remains silent and finally I think this is the key — just to be with him without filling the space with so much talking. I miss the days when we were in the moment — all feeling and none of the overthinking.

Alex settles a little deeper into his lounger, resting his hand next to mine. His fingertips draw gentle circles on the crisp white canvas of my cushion. He draws closer and closer until his smallest fingertip is grazing my thigh with every pass. Shudders of excitement course through me as I try to control my rattling heart. This doesn't feel right — right here, right now, doing this with him — but I can't bring myself to put a stop to it either. Something has been pulsing between us — first the night in Miami and then the emails we've been passing back and forth all week . . .

I've been doing my best to avoid him since he came home on Friday — my goal is to be neither seen nor heard, and I've been taking it to heart. I'm aware that this is a delicate situation and that it's not my place to intervene any more than I already have. I've already regretted my *maybe it's time to hire an attorney* email a hundred times — not because I don't think it isn't time — but because I don't want him to think I *care* if he hires a lawyer or not. I don't want to play any role in the dissolution of this marriage — at least not obviously.

I remember a silly line from one of my favorite movies: *the man may be the head of the household, but the woman is the neck, and she can turn the head whichever way she pleases.* I've found that the art of loving and the art of war are two sides of the same coin. Love can feel like a battle zone on its worst days and with enough patience and planning I'll usurp the Queen of this household from her throne before she even realizes the war has started. Gen has left herself and her family vulnerable to an ambush.

"I've been thinking about your last email—" Alex breaks the silence.

"Yeah?" I breathe, my eyes falling closed as I sigh softly. "Maybe I shouldn't have sent it."

"I'm glad you did." His palm grazes my thigh and remains there. "I like knowing how you're feeling." His hand slides over the top of my bare thigh and goosebumps break out in his wake. His hand settles at my inner thigh and I find that everything in me wants him to move just a little bit closer. "I can't predict the future but . . ." he starts, "we'll be okay, right?"

I nod because I don't have words. How could I? Were we ever okay? I'm not even sure anymore. I'm here for him, but my experience with this family has been so much *more* than I expected in every way. I didn't expect to love the kids — I didn't expect to fall for him all over again — I didn't expect to be filling the role of a mother as well as a wife because the real one spends her days drunk on champagne and sadness by the pool. Gen has been practically catatonic since I got here — is this how it's always been? I swallow down the painful ball in my throat when I think of my own reckless mother. She could hardly take care of herself all of those years. I'm still not sure if living with her would have been better than being in foster care, but it doesn't matter now. None of it does. Only this moment matters. With *him.*

"I haven't been able to stop thinking about that night in Miami." His fingertips trace the top of my thigh and then travel up the curve of my torso and land at my neck. "We should do it again."

I turn, eyes holding his as I nod slowly. Before I can even register what he's doing, his lips are on mine. My heart thunders as I turn into him, my arms around his neck as he hauls me closer. His hands are suddenly everywhere, and before I know it I'm in his lap and my legs are straddling his thighs. His lips cover my skin, hands moving over my body like he knows me better than himself.

I try not to lose myself — he feels so good, so right. The humid air hangs thick like a blanket around us, so oppressive and heady it feels like it's magnetized. His large hands cup my ass cheeks, pulling me closer into him as lips and hands explore skin. Anxiety rattles to life as I think about getting caught. What would happen if Gen walked out right now? Would she scream or cry or kill me? Maybe all of the above? Alex doesn't seem to be phased though — he touches me as if he's chosen me. As if I'm his and always have been. I think back on his email:

I'm thinking of ending things . . .

This is it. This is what I came for. It's all happening — with every day here I get a little closer to attaining my goal and making my dream come true.

"Alex—" My breaths come shallow and quick. "We shouldn't — not here."

He groans but relaxes his grip on me. "Sure."

It takes everything in me to unpeel myself from him when every part of me wants to be tangled up with him like a pretzel.

I stand, straighten my rumpled t-shirt and then swallow down the awkward silence. I glance his way briefly and find that his eyes are closed, his chin turned up to the sky. He looks . . . tortured by something. It feels like I should say something, but what it is I'm not sure. So I don't say anything. I move away from him, sucking in calming breaths of air as I create distance between us. The closer I get to the pool house the hotter Gen's letter burns in my pocket. I'm slipping it out of its hiding spot and then run my finger along the edge to break the seal. I sit down on the loveseat in the living area and train my eyes on Gen's tidy handwriting.

I skim down the lines until I reach a phrase that stands out — *employment references* — and then another — *Child Protective Services*. My heart sinks.

The following paragraphs relay the little information Gen has managed to glean about me from a few quick internet searches. The most damaging seems to be that she knows where I come from — she claims to have a report from Child Protective Services that includes claims of sexual abuse. How could she possibly have found all of this out? I assumed all of the records were hidden because I was underage. I guess access is just another thing that wealthy people have that evades the rest of us.

I cringe, realizing if the people in Palm Beach knew the real me, I'd never survive it. I blink away a memory buried in the deepest recesses of my mind. From the beginning it's been me or them, and at the end of the day, I will always choose me.

I never told Alex any of these things about me, not even when we met before because I'd left it all behind. The past remains in the past, I wouldn't have the heart or the hope to take another step forward if it didn't.

My fingers start to tremble as I read the last line — Gen plans on firing me and hiring a new au pair. This can't happen — not yet. I'm not ready. My plan hasn't come to fruition yet. I need just a few more days. I need Gen or Alex to file for a divorce — I need the split to be permanent so I can have what has always been mine.

My breathing turns ragged as I realize all I've worked for is about to turn to ash in the span of a moment. Gen must think it's me that Alex is having an affair with — planting the lingerie in his overnight bag backfired — I needed her to assume that it was someone else, someone at work maybe. For my plan to work Gen needs to believe it's *anyone* but me.

I can't let her reveal anymore — if Alex knows where I came from . . . if he knows I lied . . . well, everything else I've said is in question. And if Gen's concerns have Alex questioning my integrity he'll block me from his life and never look back. I'll do whatever it takes to prevent that from happening.

I shoot up from the loveseat and move on smooth strides out of the pool house and across the patio to the main house. Alex is already gone. I follow the soft yellow glow of the café lights that are strung from the pergola and fence to the back door. It's a calm night — only the insects and frogs singing splinter the silence. The rage that shook my system just moments ago has evaporated to a quiet calm knowing. I've been here before and I will not let anyone uproot my life by revealing my true upbringing when I've only just made it this far.

I enter the peaceful house and climb the stairs just like I've done a hundred times in the days before now. I blink away flashbacks of my childhood triggered by Gen's letter: maggots in the sink and dead flies dusting the window sills. Broken toilets that didn't flush for weeks and a pantry lined with more vodka bottles than food. Painful memories clutch at my throat like a vice wrapped in barbed wire. With every step I breathe a little deeper, clear my head a little more, strengthen my resolve to survive. I will always survive.

By the time I'm upstairs, I see the door to Gen's bedroom cracked. I open it silently, stepping into her bedroom to find the one thing I least expected. *Him.*

Why is *he* here? According to Gen they haven't slept together since the kids were born. So why did he leave me on the patio and climb directly into her bed? Anger and hurt swirl in a vicious tornado inside of me as tears blur my vision. I blink them away. I suck in deep breaths. I try to control the unbearable fury that's throttling my system.

I can't. I can't. I can't do this anymore.

I move closer to the man I love — the man I've always loved. Memories of our time together flood my mind. How could he have thrown me away so carelessly? Am I that easy to get over? It suddenly feels like my experience of *us* was night and day from his. In his eyes, I saw my future. I thought he did too, I thought he saw us together. *Just like old times.*

Despair twists my intestines in knots as I think about our time together. Every loving caress, kind word, and thoughtful gesture floods me with tidal waves of heartbreak. I missed him every day that we spent apart. I needed his love like air to

158

breathe and he never needed mine at all. That's where I went wrong: *needing* someone. Never again will I make that mistake.

My stomach burns and twists with a memory I've spent my entire life trying to forget.

Hot tears cover my cheeks as I heat another microwave dinner. I've eaten three of them today because it's the only food in the house. It's Christmas Day. While my classmates are opening presents and eating home-cooked meals with their families, I am here. Alone. I opened my single present I found under the miniature tabletop tree this morning — a donation from some kind soul to the Salvation Army Holiday Toy Drive. I can tell by the gift tag. My father forgot to take it off. He didn't even take the time to sign it from Santa or anything. Probably because he was high when he picked it up last night. That's the year I got a t-ball set for Christmas. I'm sure it was one of the last gifts left, so dear old Dad couldn't be choosy.

Just as the microwave dings that it's finished cooking my country-fried pork chop and gravy, my father comes stumbling down the hallway. He's naked except for the boxers that hang on his narrow hips. His eyes are shadowed and sunken — like he's had the life kicked out of him. He has, I guess. Even at ten I know he is an addict. Dad veers into the bathroom and then urinates for the next two minutes with the door open. I try to block the sound from my ears, focusing on my dinner and the new book I picked up at the library before Christmas break began.

"Ty—" I cringe when I hear his latest pop tart come stumbling down the hall. I see a billow of pink satin enter the bathroom after him. The thought of them together in intimate ways makes me want to be sick.

"Girl!" My father bellows.

I hunch on instinct, always expecting an open palm to come out of nowhere and smack me upside the head. I muster my most cheerful tone. "In here!"

"Thought I told you to fucking clean this toilet!" He saunters out, eyes glazed as they swing around the small kitchen in search of me. After a moment, he seems to gather enough focus to make me out in the shadows. All the blinds are closed because that's what he wants — sunshine gives him a headache. "You make one of those for me?"

He bends, rips the fork from my hand, stabs the floppy factory meat and takes as big a bite as he can. He drops the pork chop back in the tray. A spray of gravy covers the table and my t-shirt. *"Fucking cold in the center."*

Just like your heart, I think.

"Merry Christmas, Dad." I slather my tone with upbeat inflection.

"M'rry Chrisssmas." He slurs. Moves to the fridge. Opens a Miller Light and drinks all of it in one thirsty swallow. *"You get your gift?"*

"Yes. I love it. Thanks." I bet he doesn't even remember what he got me.

He grunts in reply.

"Gosh — it's after six p.m.? How did the day get away from us?" The pop tart simpers, dragging a red-tipped fingernail along his willowy bicep.

"I get distracted when you're naked, that's why." He does his best to send her a charming smile but it's really just smarmy. He looks like a drug addict you'd avoid eye contact with if you walked by him on the sidewalk. Because he is. I will never marry someone like him. I will never let myself be used by a man like this. A man who takes and doesn't have the capacity to give.

"I gotta get home to my kids, their dad is supposed to drop them off at six thirty, I'm gonna be late." She pecks him on the cheek. *"I'll call you later, okay, baby?"*

"Sounds good, sweetheart." He pats her ass as she shimmies down the hallway and into his bedroom. In less than a minute she's stalking back through the kitchen, torn jean shorts and dirty, cigarette-scented tank top on as she exits the house with a giggle and a wave. I want to feel bad for her, especially knowing tomorrow night he'll just have another flavor-of-the-week in his bed, but I can't bring myself to muster an ounce of empathy. She's using him, just like he is her. She's using him for attention — and she's lucky because he gives it to her. He gives her the attention he seems unable to give me.

"You have a good Christmas?" Dad flops down onto the old couch. The springs protest even under his thin frame.

"It was great." I breathe the lie as my heart splinters a little more at the edges. *"You?"*

"Fan-fucking-tastic." He lights a cigarette, takes one long draw, and then picks up his phone and makes a call. *"Hey — you got any more morphine? That shit knocked me out. I need more of it."*

I push my hands over my face as if I'm washing it with invisible soap. Washing away the agony of never being enough. The torment of competing for my father's time with an endless parade of drugs and women. Alex was better. At least I thought he was. But I guess I was living in a delusion to believe any man could stay.

I don't know where I went wrong with Alex, but I know I've invested too much in him to only come this far. My love, my energy, my youth all wasted.

Love is beautiful and painful. Life is miraculous and monstrous. I've learned both will hit you like a bullet in the back.

I don't understand how he could throw our love away. My father's selfish smirk flashes in my mind — he taught me my earliest lessons about what to expect from men — things like trust, loyalty, and honor are fickle — too much to expect from another human. All we have is ourselves.

I move closer to Alex's gentle snores and spot a prescription bottle on the nightstand. His sleeping pills. No wonder he's sleeping so soundly already. Bile rises as my mother's careless warnings rush through my mind.

Never trust a man. Never trust a man. Never trust a man.

Or a woman, I think.

I'll have to deal with Gen later, but for now, I can only focus on one step at a time. I was used by all of them, abused and then tossed away. I guess I'm not the first one to be eaten up and spit out by the rich. Betrayal thickens the blood in my veins. Bitterness and wrath chug through my system like a freight train. My mind feels like it's fraying at the edges.

My gaze lands on Alex's golf bag propped against the bureau. My feet move in that direction without my mind even making the decision to do so. I reach the bag, trailing a fingertip along the fuzzy cover of one of the irons. My heart hammers as I clutch it in my hand and pull it from its rightful place.

I take in his peaceful sleeping form, such a stark contrast to the slow-simmering rage that's climbing in my system. "Look what you made me do, Alex . . ."

CHAPTER THIRTY-FIVE

Genevieve

I swallow. My throat is dry like it's been baked in the summer sun. I lick my lips. The taste of copper. I wince. Blood. Blood. *Why blood?* My skull pounds like a champion boxer has been throwing left hooks my way all night. I lick my lips again. More copper. I run my palms over my forearms. Everything feels so cold. My eyes burn with exhaustion but I force them open anyway. My eyelashes are caked with sleep. I rub at them to free my vision.

As soon as my eyes are open I know something is very wrong.

Darkness shrouds the bedroom. Despite the fact that a fresh breeze is coming through an open window, something smells . . . *off*. The humid air is thick with the scent of a butcher's counter. My heartbeat thrums wildly as I push myself out of bed. And then I see it. A spray of blood on the lampshade. My stomach lurches. I cover my mouth as I stand, eyes scanning the bedroom. It looks like Jackson Pollock created a masterpiece in here last night. Except this isn't art. It's a horror show. Hot tears fill my eyes as I come around the end of our king bed. The first thing I see is Alex's bare foot. I drop to my knees and crawl to him, my hands reaching his ankle to find he is cold. So very cold.

"No!" I scream. "No. No. No."

I crawl around the corner of the bed, my hands covering his blood-splattered skin.

"Please, I need you," I whisper as I cling to his moonlit form. "Please."

He's wearing only his boxer briefs, one arm covering his face as if he died blocking a blow. My vision is watery and red-soaked as I glance around the room in search of some sort of clue to what happened. Terror throttles me as I think about the kids. The entire house is silent — was there an intruder? How did I survive and my husband didn't? And why is he even in here when he always sleeps in the guest bedroom?

My muscles shake with fear as I crawl over my husband's body. Rivers of tears cut through the blood that cakes my face. How did I survive a blood bath?

It's then I see it.

The golf club.

A 9-iron covered in blood lies next to Alex's body. Nearly hiding under the bed, I almost missed it. I swallow, sure that this is the weapon used to bludgeon my husband to death.

My fingers shake as I trace the fuzzy cover. It's then I focus on my own fingers — caked beneath all of my nails is a thick layer of maroon. My knuckles are dry and caked with blood, my creamy silk pajamas are soaked as if I swam at the beach during a red tide. "Alex—"

I bite down on my bottom lip before I press myself off the floor and walk to the en suite bathroom. My fingers quake as I flip on the light. I crush my eyes closed as I step in front of the mirror, not ready to see my reflection. As soon as I see it, I know there will be no going back. I swallow once, muster a deep breath, and then allow my eyes to flutter open.

"Oh no." I cry and press my palms to my red-stained cheeks. I look like I stepped off the set of a horror movie.

Blood cakes my lips, my eyelids, my eyebrows. It looks like I've painted my face in red paint save for the flesh-toned rivers where my tears cut a divide.

"I . . . I . . ." I'm stumbling out of the bathroom now, bloody footprints leaving a trail as I go. I'll need Adeline to help me clean this — and then it occurs to me. *Where is Adeline?* I need to call 911. I need to find the children. I need to wash my face and hands and maybe even take a shower. I'm covered in blood that's not my own. From what I can tell I don't have a single scratch, nothing hurts, how did this happen and I didn't wake up? How was I here while my husband was murdered right under my nose? My gaze hovers on the doorway as I realize one thing is very wrong with this scene.

There's so much blood, and I'm leaving my own footprints everywhere . . . so where are the killer's prints?

Violent shakes pummel me as I realize what's wrong here. There's no sign of an entry or exit by anyone else. No footprints. No blood on the doorknob. It's as if . . . whoever did this is still *here*. I rush back to the bathroom on the hunt for anything that wasn't here before. It's then I see it. A bag from the pharmacy. I tear the paper bag open and find my anxiety medication waiting for me. I blink when I read the label. Something the size of a stone forms in my throat and causes a slow ache. Fresh tears well in my eyes. I lift the bottle, turning it in my hands as it occurs to me that it's been nearly eight weeks that I've been out of this medication.

The pharmacist must've called Alex to let him know our refills were ready and he must've picked them up on the way home from Miami on Friday. Why didn't he tell me? Or maybe he did, I think, and it's just one more hole in my memory. I press my hands on the vanity and push myself to standing. My reflection in the mirror sends chills through me. I'm covered in the blood of the man I love. I think back to the letter I wrote him — the one he never replied to, even though he took the time to reply to Adeline over the course of many days and many emails. He wasn't willing to talk *to* me, but he sure was eager to talk *about* me.

I open the prescription bottle and shake out a little white pill. Vilazoplam. How could so much — the very safety of my family — depend on this tiny little combination of compounds and chemicals? I've known for years that the medications that have been treating my disorder have a tendency of leaving holes in my short-term memory but now I know that the withdrawal from them is worse than when they're chugging through my system daily. In withdrawal, everything feels hazy and spotty. Now it's clear why I have no memory of Adeline explaining that she was leaving that day at the beach. Why I have no memory of . . . *anything*.

I swallow the tiny tab down without water just as a flash of last night comes to me. The emails. The lingerie. The patio make-out session with Adeline. The rage. So much rage. The golf club. Alex's shattered cheekbone. A flood of blood gushing from his ear. A ferocious gash across his eyebrow that left a sickening crunch echoing in my ears.

I force the memory to the back of my skull, never to be accessed again.

I think back to the last time we were in this place, unsure of how to make sense of the new reality we'd found ourselves in. I wasn't always upfront with Alex about my mental health. I didn't tell him that the first time I went on anxiety medications when I was fifteen was because my sadness devolved into psychosis. I never explained how my sense of self can sometimes fragment in an effort to cope under stress. Would he have been understanding if I'd described what it felt like the first time I split? I've adapted to solo trips through hell over the years, inviting company seems counterintuitive.

Since that day I've thought of these stupid little pills like friends. My very best friends. The friends that keep me sane in an insane world. But could I really have done this? Is Adeline no more than a boogeyman made up by my mind to cope with the constant stress of motherhood? I can't trust my own brain, these little white pills have been in my life longer than my husband . . . well, former husband now. Now, I am a widow.

I think again of the lingerie. The plane tickets to Fiji. The lie about the golf trip to Phoenix. The night in Little Havana. Alex must have assumed when I brought his file to Miami that I was looking to recapture the passion between us — the little black dress and heels and so much make-up. It really was like old times for both of us, only it was Adeline that night — Adeline looking to connect with the man she fell in love with.

I think of the night we came home early from the getaway at The Breakers — Albertine all alone for hours while I imagined Adeline to be watching her — while Alex thought the new nanny had everything under control.

A flash of a memory pierces the calm as a vision of his moaning form comes to me, groggy with sleep and shock, after I land the first blow with the golf club. I look down and feel nothing — not love, not hate, not anything in the space between. This must be what the end feels like, I think now. There are people who work through the hard times, couples who fight for one another and push forward for the children. But what happens when you have nothing left to fuel the fire? How do you go on when you have nothing left to give? Life would be so much easier if I could only love them like they needed me to.

I push my hands over my face, viscous blood smearing into my hairline. The face looking back at me is worn and lifeless, lined with worry and resentment. I look like my mother, right before she left me for the night to meet another man.

"Maman!" Albertine's call echoes through the second level.

My heartbeat rattles to a halt. She is here. She is alive. And now I am all she has.

"Adeline!" I call out of habit. And then I remember.

There is no Adeline. There is only me. Adeline was only a figment of my mind — an imaginary friend with the power to ruin lives.

I cringe, tears of fear blurring my vision. What does this mean for me and my babies? I've just stolen their father from them . . . or have I?

I gulp down the awareness of my next steps. If the police are called, a fragile mental health defense will not hold up in court. I will be tried and convicted of murder and then the kids — where would they go? Into foster care? I made them. My body their first home. The idea that someone could take them away from me is enough to crush what's left of me.

I have no memory of Adeline telling me she was leaving that day at the beach with the kids because it didn't happen.

I have no memory of my husband's murder because it didn't happen.

It was Adeline.

It was *always* Adeline.

I need to believe this with every fiber of my being if I'm going to carry on with my life. The only chance the kids and I have to move on is if I believe this singular fact: It. Was. Adeline.

I make quick work of washing my face, scrubbing the horror from my skin just like I've scrubbed it from my memory.

Another moment later and I'm walking down the hall in the direction of Albertine's room. I've changed my clothes and pulled my hair back into a sleek ponytail, careful to cover the bald spot on the back of my head. I'm sure Albertine won't notice that caked in every pore and follicle are trace remains of her father.

I swallow down the dread and bile that threatens to climb up my throat as I twist Albertine's doorknob. I push in the door and find her cross-legged on the floor, tears welling in her big brown eyes. She looks so much like her father right now it gnaws at my insides. My stomach churns and I have to control the urge to throw up all over my daughter's wool rug.

"Who locked me in my room?!" Albertine cries.

"I don't know, baby." I bend and pull her into my arms, stroking her back as warm tears fall down my cheeks. "It must have been an accident." I finally say in explanation. "Sometimes accidents just happen, you know that, right?"

Albertine nods, hiccups, and then jumps from her spot on the floor and darts around me and out of the room. Relief courses through me when she turns in the opposite direction of my bedroom — where her father lays lifeless and bloody on the floor — and instead zips down the stairs to the main floor. I follow her quickly, realizing Adeline must have locked Albertine's door out of safety last night before . . . well, before the unthinkable happened.

It's tricky — knowing you are two people but lying to your mind that you are only one. For this act to succeed, on some level, I must believe there is an Adeline that slayed my husband — and on the surface I must commit to the lie that they ran away together — an act of betrayal that occurred right under my nose. Now, I must believe in make-believe to secure my safety and freedom. The mind is a funny thing — the lengths it will go to protect itself from harm are extraordinary and sometimes outlandish. Sometimes downright fantasy . . . but isn't that all life is? A hologram of shapes and colors that our brain interprets to help us get along? A fantastical adventure in make-believe, no different than *Alice in Wonderland*, except my wonderland is less wonderful and more horror movie. We all tell ourselves lies to get along. Life is a dream and meaning is what we make of it. And in this life, I choose this lie.

What happened was wrong, but just like I explained to Albertine, sometimes accidents happen. Foolish, unpredictable, tragic accidents.

"Can I have avocado toast, Maman?" Albertine shrieks when I find her in the kitchen. She's bouncing up and down and clapping her hands together. She has so much infectious joy considering she lives in a house of horrors.

"That sounds delicious. Hey — honey — how about you start calling me Mommy? No more Maman — unless you like to of course."

"Okay, Mommy." Albertine smiles sweetly.

Tears jump into my eyes. "I love when you call me that." I pull her into a hug. "Whaddya say we have breakfast by the pool and turn on a movie?" I say, snapping back to reality as

I realize I'll need to buy myself enough time to clean up the bedroom without Albertine noticing I'm gone and while the baby still sleeps.

"Ooh, can we watch *The Christmas Chronicles?*" Albertine is gleeful.

I smile at her request for Christmas in Spring *again*. I wish I could escape from reality for just a moment too. But right now, I have a murder scene to clean up.

I start with the Persian wool rug. Sixty thousand dollars of hand-knotted luxury and now Alex's blood soaks the ivory wool fibers. I'll never get it clean. I drape our bedsheet over his body and then spray all of it with bleach paying extra attention to the area next to his form. After forty-five minutes of scrubbing, I groan, tossing my scrubber and pink rubber gloves in the water bucket and then shoving the frame of our king bed to one side. Once it's off the rug, I begin rolling from the edge until it's as tightly wound around him as I can get it. It hurts my heart to throw this rug away, but I don't have a choice. I can't think of anything else to do with him and hauling a grown man down the stairs seems just about impossible. I also don't want to leave a trail of DNA through the house, so I open the double doors that lead to the balcony that overlooks the patio and pool. With a few heaves, I pull the rug over to the balcony and leave him there. I'll dispose of him and the rug over the side later once Albertine is done with her movie. I'll have to think about what to do with him after that, but right now, I have evidence to get rid of.

I sigh, turning back to my bloody bedroom. I begin with wiping down every surface, from the double nightstands to the bureaus. The windows and trim get my attention next, and then I move to the walls. I press my lips together with exhaustion as a slow ache radiates through my neck and shoulder blades. I pause to rub my muscles. I'll be recovering from the last twenty-four hours for a week at least. I make a mental note to schedule a massage wherever Albertine, Laurent and I land next. Then, I flip on a playlist of acoustic covers and then begin the agonizing process of soaping down every inch of wall and ceiling in this room.

By the time I'm finished, my head is swimming with the bleach fumes but the walls are clean. They'll still need to be painted before we sell, but in the meantime I'll spend the next few days touching up the faint pink droplets as best I can. I consider how nice it would be to hire painters to finish the job for me, but I can't risk it. Once I'm satisfied with the walls, I move to the floor, mopping with a mixture of Pine Sol and bleach. Even with the windows and balcony doors open and the ceiling fan on high, the air in the room is thick with fumes. And then it hits me that I've overlooked the ceiling fan, so I flip the switch and wait until the blades slowly stop. I push the bed back into place and then stand on it to wipe down every part of the fan that I can reach. And then I step back in the doorway and survey my work. It's been two hours and I haven't even started on the bathroom.

But first, I need to check on Albertine.

It takes me less than fifteen minutes to wash myself up and then get the kids down for naps. We even read a book and talk about places she'd like to visit during summer break. I drop a kiss on both of her cheeks, promising soon we'll visit Paris and Milan, and then I get back to work.

I spend another three hours scrubbing down the bathroom and then going back over every last corner of our bedroom while I think about how I have to get ahead of this story if I'm going to make it work for me. I have to plant the right seeds to secure my freedom. The kids and I deserve a new chapter and I'll do whatever it takes to make sure we get it.

CHAPTER THIRTY-SIX

"You wouldn't believe what Alex did—" I finger the pearls that clutch my throat like a noose.

The other wives pause. Four sets of eyes land on me.

"He ran off with the help . . ." I begin before a cascade of tears wash my cheeks. "He and the au pair I hired ran off together."

Four hands decorated with Cartier rings the size of boulders cover lips perfectly plumped with filler.

"Oh no — I'm so sorry." Starts the chorus of condolences.

"Apparently they knew each other before we even met." I lie. "I'm afraid it was all planned and—" I affect heartbreak — "I guess I never really knew him at all." I don't expect any of these women will be suspicious that they never met the au pair because they're all too self-involved to think about what's been happening under my roof.

"Oh, honey," Marissa purrs. "I'm so sorry. How did you find out?"

I let her question linger for a long, pregnant moment. I resent that she's being so nosy and putting me in the spotlight in front of the other mommy zombies like this.

"I woke up Sunday morning in my bed alone. They just . . . *vanished.*" I sob again, shoulders shaking with an oncoming panic attack.

"Vanished?" Hannah asks, one perfectly pointed eyebrow raised.

"Just gone." I confirm, suppressing a shiver.

"Hm." Juanita plucks a green grape into her mouth and chews. Her eyes hold mine and I have to shove away the thought that she doesn't believe me. She has no reason not to. I've been talking about the au pair for two months — I'd also mentioned my suspicions about Alex's infidelities while he's away all week in Miami. At least I think I did.

This should all line up for them. So why do I get the feeling that they don't believe me? A small voice reminds me that I probably just have a mild case of paranoia. Post-traumatic stress too.

"That's so awful — after everything?" Chimes someone.

"What a no-good rat." Another huff.

"We're so sorry, Genevieve, if we can do anything at all—" Marissa adds.

I shake my head to cut them all off. "No. I just need a new start. That's why I called you here — I think I'm going to put the house up for sale. Too many memories." I wipe at manufactured tears. "It's awful because I think I caught them the night they left on the patio kissing. It was so dark I couldn't tell from the house, but now that I think about it, I'm sure it was . . ."

"Oh, honey." Marissa pats my hand in sympathy. "Gosh, you never really know a person, right?"

I nod sadly, fighting the twitch of a smile that threatens my lips.

"How is Albertine handling it?" Hannah asks.

"She doesn't know yet — she thinks he just went back to Miami early. How do you tell a child her daddy left her to be with a younger woman?" I sniff. "I'm sorry to ruin your morning ladies, forgive me. I just can't think about this anymore.

Does anyone need a mimosa refill?" I stand and before anyone can answer I'm already moving toward the main house. As soon as I reach the door I duck inside and press my back to the wall. I cover my face with my hands and allow a hot wave of emotion to wash over me.

Being back on the medication for the last two days after going cold turkey for nearly two months is taking a toll. I didn't expect the side effects to return, the extreme emotional swings and forgetfulness is worse than before, but thankfully, at least so far, the medication has controlled the splitting.

Adeline hasn't been here since the night Alex was murdered.

I know it's against the doctor's orders, but I was so concerned Adeline might come back before I had a chance to clean up the bloody scene and get rid of the body that I took an extra dose two hours after the first. And I've been doubling my dose in the days since. So far, so good. But only time will tell if Adeline is really gone forever.

"Poor thing — can you believe it? After everything her husband just up and leaves her for a younger woman?" Hannah's voice carries across the patio to my ears.

"Gen told me once that they have an iron-clad prenup — she said she invested her modeling money well and now just the dividends pay more than his yearly salary," Juanita says knowingly.

"She's lucky — she gets to keep her millions — can you imagine if he'd left her for a younger woman *and* wiped out all her cash?" Fawn murmurs.

I've been grinding my teeth so forcefully pain radiates through my jaw as I listen to them. The nosy gossips have no idea what they're saying. I clamp down on the memories pushing at the edges of my mind.

There were never any runway shows. Instead there were men. So many men. *Walking for Gucci in Milan never happened.* Instead there was running for my life barefoot down Ocean Avenue at dawn. *Promises of fashion shows and luxury ad campaigns fell from their lips as their hands crawled across my skin and I swallowed down tears.* Wealthy men. Luxury parties. Massages with benefits. I blink as I remember nights of endless pain, sometimes bruises, choking on fear. So much fear. There were never any lucrative investments with high-paying dividends or bank accounts that overflowed with cash. It was all an elaborate figment of my mind.

I shove the harsh reality of my past back where it belongs — locked in the basement of my mind. I refuse to allow where I come from to control my future like a curse. I may not have had a modeling career like I lead these women and Alex to believe, but I was blessed the day Alex proposed to me at our little bungalow in Miami. Sometimes I think he was my good karma after a lifetime of suffering. Alex's presence gave me warm feelings of safety and security that I'd never felt before that moment. Alex loved me out of the gutter, literally, because the moment I said *yes* to his proposal, I never took another escort job again. I led Alex to believe that I wanted to quit modeling to start a family, that the late nights and the days spent traveling took their toll on our budding new life. But really, I was dying inside trying to stay afloat with Hugo and his little black book of wealthy men. Spending time with them for even an hour, no matter how good the money was, made me feel like a fraud and a fake when I went home to Alex, washed away another man's sweat from my skin, then crawled into bed and tried desperately not to cry myself to sleep in his arms.

Every time I came home from a date, I grew more determined to be the woman Alex deserved. I gave him all of me back then I was so desperate for him to keep me. I gave him my life and then, I took his. My jaw aches with the incessant grinding of my teeth. A new tic I've picked up as I process the grief.

"She looks like a mess—" the judgment in Fawn's voice shakes me from my dark thoughts — "I've never seen Genevieve so . . . *undone.*"

"Fawn please — can you imagine if Jerry left? You'd be a basket case too." Marissa defends me. "Especially so soon after losing the baby."

My vision fades to black as my mind cycles on Marissa's last words.

Especially after losing the baby . . . What does she mean?

CHAPTER THIRTY-SEVEN

"Albertine, honey?" A headache is still pressing at the edges of my skull thirty minutes later. I have so many questions my brain hurts and Alex isn't here to answer any of them.

"Yes, Mommy?" Albertine looks up at me with round, trusting eyes.

I swallow, afraid to even say the next words out loud. But I have to. I can't stop thinking about what the other wives said. "Honey . . ." I drop to her level and plant a palm on her shoulders. "Do you remember the baby?"

Her gaze cuts away from mine. "Yes. I remember him."

It hurts me to ask her this next question. It kills me that I don't remember. I've resorted to borrowing the memories of a five-year-old to fill in the holes in my own short-term memory. "Do you remember where your brother went?"

"Yes." She nods, gaze still trained on the floor between us.

"Where did he go?" I ask.

"In the ground."

My heart somersaults. I'm afraid to ask *why*. I'm afraid that my little girl might tell me that *I* did this — that I am responsible for my son's death too. And what's worse — I'm afraid that no matter what she tells me I won't believe her.

I've come to believe the line between a lie and a mental health lapse is a thin one.

And after the night Alex . . . *left* . . . well, I'd be lying if I didn't admit that I'm terrified of what else I might be capable of. My only saving grace is that this only happened when I went off the medications for weeks, my anxiety spiraling and the visions increasingly harder to handle until . . . well, until Adeline came along. It's like some people perceive reality differently than others, and these little tiny tablets help my brain to catch up with everyone else's.

I look down at Albertine, her tiny little fingers pretzeled together with anxiety. She can feel how tense I've been. She's so perceptive. My breath catches when I realize that I am not the best example of a mother to raise her. Maybe deep down I hoped Alex could keep me tethered to reality but in the end, life doesn't work like that. I married him to escape myself, but there is no escape. Outrunning my mind is an impossible task.

I think for the first time since Alex . . . *left* . . . that it would be so easy to move on from here. One last obstacle on the path to freedom. But will I ever really be free? I'll always be tethered to her. To him. To these pills. To my story.

My father's whisky-soaked breath on my skin. His friends leering at me and begging for a taste in exchange for giving my father free drugs. The way my mother's last husband crushed her cheekbone with a beer bottle one of the last times I ever saw her before the state removed me from her care and placed me in the hands of my father at twelve. The Breakers. Massages. Wealthy Men. Penthouses. More men. More money. So many men. So much darkness. The list of Miami's most eligible bachelors that I carried around for months holding onto just a glimmer of hope . . . And then the light shone in: Alexandre. My love. Freedom. Palm Beach. The kids. Now.

Albertine's shoulders start to quiver as she covers her face with her palms in a gesture I do so often now. She must have learned it from me: the mental breakdown 101 starter kit.

"I'm sorry, honey. We don't have to talk about your brother." I soothe her shaking form. She crawls into my arms and holds me tightly. I pat her back, swallowing down the pain of not knowing what happened to my son in favor of keeping her safe. Even if it means that we never talk about what happened again.

What if the truth opens a Pandora's box for both of us that I'm not ready for? That I may never be ready for? I can't upset the delicate balance I've found myself in and telling anyone would certainly do that. And if anyone suspected there was even a chance that I could do this to my husband the first thing they'd do is take Albertine away from me. But who else could raise my daughter better than me? Certainly no one in Palm Beach or Pahokee or in the system. I sacrificed my livelihood to be her mother — to give Alex the family I thought we both wanted. In the end . . . maybe neither of us knew what we really wanted.

Or maybe Alex did and it was just me that was the problem. I'm still not sure. I don't think I ever will be.

I think of my own neglectful parents. How easy it was to walk away from them for my survival. Would Albertine be better off without me? Would she be better served by the foster care system? Would one of the other wives be a better fit to be her mother than me?

"Mommy?" Albertine hiccups as she untucks herself from the crook of my neck.

"Yeah, baby?"

Albertine's next question lands like a death blow. "Can I call Daddy tonight?"

I sigh and crush my eyes closed as a vein of resentment runs through me. It takes everything in me not to say *Daddy ran off with the help*.

Instead I opt for: "He's busy with work, honey, but I'll ask if he has time."

She nods. "Okay. Can we go to the playground today?"

"Yeah, baby, I just have to take care of a few things first. Can you sit here and be good until I come back to get you?"

She smiles widely. "Yes, Mommy. I'll be very, very good. I promise."

"Good, baby. I'm so proud of you." I pull her into one last hug. "I love you to the moon and back, don't ever forget that, okay?"

She nods, holds my face between her hands and then pecks me on the forehead. It's a gesture I often do to her and something that warms my heart that she's returning the comfort. Something in her knows. Just like I know this isn't over yet, she knows nothing will ever be the same for us. We only have each other now. Her and Mommy against the world. A chill runs through me at the thought.

I still don't know if I'm ready.

CHAPTER THIRTY-EIGHT

I'm not ready. I'm not ready.

My hand hovers on the door at the end of the hall.

I'm not ready. I'm not ready.

I breathe deeply, bracing myself for what's to come.

I'm not ready. I'm not ready.

I twist and push. And then my heart falls.

The scent of baby powder hangs in the air. It's as if he was just here, babbling and cooing as his diaper is changed.

Everything is spotless. No dust lingers on the crib or changing table. A framed photo of Alex and Laurent on the day he was born catches my breath. Everything I've lost contained in a single 4x6 frame. Tears jump into my eyes. Time seemed to make him a brighter version of the man I married. And as the years passed, the life only dimmed in my eyes. I yearned for his lightness, for just a little of him to rub off on me. I needed him to chase away the clouds. But every time he left for work the storms descended despite all of my best efforts.

I open the top drawer of the bureau and find a stack of swim diapers waiting patiently for the next time Laurent goes swimming.

Except there won't be a next time.

I pick up a small stuffed bunny and hold it in my arms, inhaling the sweet baby scent of my son.

And then an unwelcome flashback chugs through my mind. I drop to my knees as pain crashes through me. Waves of grief swallow my sanity. I remember, but I don't want to. I desperately want to forget. I crush my eyes closed, willing the memories to evaporate as quickly as they came.

Splashing. Jumping. Screams.

"No." I gasp as my heart cleaves.

Splashing. Shouting. Stillness.

"Please." I hold my palms over my ears as if that will prevent the memories from getting in.

Blue water. Blue tiles. Blue toes.

"No, no, no." I beg for the visions to stop. I need my pills. I need to forget. I can't get lost in the pain. I won't survive it. Most things are survivable, but not this. I don't believe anyone can recover from the death of a child.

I slump on the floor, curling into the fetal position as I clutch Laurent's tiny bunny against my chest.

"I don't know. I don't know. I don't know." I remember repeating when Alex asked how this happened.

Regrets descend, crushing my hope. I know how this happened.

I was overwhelmed. I was exhausted. Alex was away all week at work and I . . . *forgot.* I fell asleep and he died and then losing him killed me too. Losing him killed all of us.

Life drained from my eyes with every passing day after, replaced by hardened anger and bitterness. In the absence of hope, anger gave me the strength to go on. Helped me maintain the fragile structure of daily life, weaving all the threads together so that sadness didn't take over everything. I wanted to hate someone for the death of my son. God for giving me life and then taking it away. Alex for being gone all week. Albertine for distracting me. Or do I only have myself to blame? In the end it's all of that and a lot more, I guess.

Hot tears cover my cheeks as blankets of blue violets flood my vision. Spring in South Florida used to be my favorite time of year. But now, I think of blue violets as the same shade of Laurent's tiny toes when I pulled his lifeless form from the pool. I press my eyes closed in a silent prayer of relief. Blue violets lined the edges of his tiny grave. Coffins should never be made this small, I remember thinking. No being, so innocent and pure, should lose their life before they've had a chance to become who they'll be. Before they've even spoken their first word. The dreams I dreamed for him the day I pushed him into this world sank like a stone the moment Laurent took his last breath.

Accidents happen. Accidents happen. Accidents happen. Alex had murmured on repeat as he rubbed my back, my shoulders shaking while we walked away from the cemetery. I haven't been the same since the day we buried my son. Alex, on my insistence, drove back to Miami for work, and I drove to Albertine's school to pick her up.

That was the day I met Adeline.

Laurent's first birthday.

The day we put Laurent in the ground.

The day I lost myself and Adeline came to the rescue.

Realization sweeps through me as I sit with the fact that another unspeakable trauma instigated another split, leaving me confused in the surreal reality of a dissociated state. Genevieve couldn't function anymore, so Adeline saved the day. If just one thing had been different, would I still be standing here today? If I'd insisted that Alex go home with me the day of our son's funeral, would Adeline still have arrived? If I'd insisted that Alex pick up Albertine at school that day, would my mind have cultivated a new personality to carry the weight that I could no longer bear? The truth is, I believe Adeline would have been waiting in the wings, making herself known when the time was right — the next time Alex left for Miami. And the other truth: I didn't want him with me then. I didn't want anyone — I wanted to be alone with my pain. I wanted to sit in my sadness and marinate in the hurt. I needed to heal and I couldn't do it with him — but I'm not sure I could do it without him either. And now I'll have to.

I gasp when another blow of regret sweeps through me.

With Adeline came Laurent. Through Adeline, I could live in a reality of my own making — where my baby was still alive and thriving. Crawling and cooing and crying and perfectly alive. I could live in a suspended reality where I didn't do this — where I'm not responsible for the death of my son. A world where I am not the monster. They say parenthood is a matter of living with your heart outside your body — everything you love is exposed and raw and vulnerable to all the evil that exists in the world — but what happens when you are the evil? When the very womb that gave life also took it away?

While I was lost in my grief these last few months, my baby came back to me. And my baby had the perfect mother in Adeline — attentive and nurturing and so very *not* resentful — everything I was not.

Adeline was my second chance.

And then the murder happened.

CHAPTER THIRTY-NINE

I drag the tip of my finger along the slipcovered sofa in the pool house. I've found myself out here a lot in the last day, my mind replaying everything from a new perspective. As if my conscious mind can't fathom reality so my unconscious keeps pulling me here, in search of any evidence that I am wrong. That Adeline was real and responsible for the unraveling of my life.

But just my luck, the place is untouched.

It's just as I left it because no guest has ever stayed here. It's pristine. The throw pillows with the blue seashell print are perfectly perched on the sofa. Clean cupboards and a sink that's never seen a dirty dish sparkle back at me. The bathroom lacks any toiletries, and the double bed that sits at the center of the single bedroom has been stripped of all bedding. Only a cheap plastic cover protects the mattress. With every step I take, I have to fight the despair that comes with my new reality.

Last night I checked Alex's email and found an invoice from the Audi dealership for brake repairs last Saturday. He must've taken the Audi to get fixed after my accident in the azaleas without saying anything to me. Or he did, and it's just another hole in my Swiss cheese memory. He was so very good and I can't shake the feeling that I ruined him. I tried to be what I thought he wanted, but the truth remains that he always deserved better than me. A pretender from Pahokee trying to swim with the sharks in Palm Beach. I was never cut out for this life — so what if I'd told him that? What if I'd confessed that none of this felt like the dream we planned together so many years ago?

My mind and I wander back to the main house in a daze. Sadness has stolen my will to live. I can't bear to be in this home we built together without him to share it with. I climb the stairs to the second floor and drag my feet the last few steps into our bedroom. *My* bedroom now. I walk right into the en suite bathroom and open the vanity. I take out a prescription bottle of Xanax and pop one, swallow it without water, and then on impulse, pop another. Forgetting feels better than grief, at least if I'm numb I can get through the day without a breakdown.

I move back into the room and as if an unseen gravitational pull draws me, I go to Alex's bureau and open the top drawer. The first thing that catches my eye is a soft pink envelope the size of a greeting card. A slow frown pulls my lips when I turn it over and find *Sugar* written in Alex's tight scrawl.

It's for me.

I open the seal and pull out a simple card with a beach umbrella sketched on it. *See you in paradise . . .* is printed in a fancy scroll across the top. With tears in my eyes, I open the card to find a long, handwritten letter from Alex.

It begins with a confession.

I've been keeping a secret,

There is no golf trip to Phoenix. It's just going to be you and me in Fiji, Sugar. Fawn says she'll keep Albertine while we're gone — our girl will have so much fun playing with Francine. She deserves fun. We all do. I've put us on the back burner for too long, Miami made me realize that I miss you and I need to make it up to you. I know you've been struggling, the grief has been hard on all of us, but most especially you. Hopefully Fiji is a fresh start. I love you now and forever.

Love, Alex

A lightning bolt of pain stabs me. My body spins. I lean on the drawers to steady myself. Anguish cuts like a knife. Something that feels like panic overcomes me as my lungs collapse under the weight of this pain. Alex still loved me. How could I have been so very wrong about everything? My anxiety and insecurity woven together into such a neat knot I couldn't decipher where one ended and the other began. Panic and pain and trauma led me down a rabbit hole so deep I couldn't see my way out. And without my medications to keep me from so much *feeling, feeling, feeling*, I lost the battle.

But we can still win the war, comes Adeline's cheerful voice.

She's right though. I have to get through this for me and Albertine. We struggled to connect before, but I've taken all that was good from her and I must make it up to her. I vow then that every day I will show her how much I love and cherish her. She will never question the depths of my love.

I press my eyelids together until my world shifts to black. I grit my teeth a few times and then release all the air from my lungs. Clamping my lips closed, I press them until they tingle with pain. Opening my eyes, I set the greeting card aside and move back to the top drawer. I pull a stack of letters from their hiding spot tucked behind the brown leather belt I gave him for his birthday years ago. We were still just dating. I think of the homemade cake I made him, a two-tier monstrosity with a poor excuse for a skyscraper piped on top in neon blue icing. I spent all afternoon making it in the kitchen of our bungalow downtown. Tears push past the barrier of my lids as I realize I'll have to tuck these memories in the basement of my mind if I have a chance at surviving.

Chin up, girl. My father's brash voice filters through the noise. *Better off thinking of a plan than blubbering like a baby. You're not a baby, are you Genny?* Six-year-old me shakes my head that I am not. *Good. Then get it together. And don't bother me again if all you're gonna do is cry.* I stuff the memory deeper, imagining that it's no longer mine.

I turn my eyes back to the stack of envelopes and find the top one flecked with bright red dots. *Blood droplets.* The top drawer of the dresser must have been open just enough to leave a spray of evidence the night of his death. I've done my best to clean every nook and crevice but the more I look, the more I find. Hiding between the wall and the crown molding, I find him. The remnants of his life reduced down to a single red pinpoint. It's taken everything in me to bleach him away over the days. I miss him. Even if this is all I have.

I glance out to the row of magnolias that line the driveway. At least he will live on, his sweet soul will bring joy each day through the life of Albertine. It's a small concession, but it's the only one I have.

I wipe at the blood splatter on the envelope but find it's dry. Of course it is. Alex has been gone for three nights. I haven't been sleeping. I spend all day with Albertine and then after she goes to bed at night, I come here.

I clean. I cry. I pray.

It's the only way I know to move on. One moment at a time.

I've been trying to piece together the moments before the nightmare began. Where did I go wrong? Could I have done anything to prevent it? What was the trigger that sent Adeline into a deadly spiral?

I think it was these letters.

I drop to the floor cross-legged and lay them out in a fan before me. I bite back the bile climbing up my throat and then open the first letter. It's addressed to *Alex* from *Your Sugar* — just like they all are.

I blink away sadness as I skim the first letter.

Adeline's handwriting is loopy and free-flowing, so different from my own.

I've missed you.
We can have what we once had.
I still love you.
This isn't the end, only a new beginning.
I'll always be there for you.

It's no wonder I killed him. I would have killed her too if I could have. Reading these letters now is a different experience than it was this weekend. This weekend I read these letters and I assumed Adeline was having an affair with my husband. Now, when read through the eyes of reality — knowing it was *me* that wrote these letters and not Adeline — brings me to a new depth of misery. I feel duped by my own brain. As if the one thing I'm meant to trust and rely on — myself, my intuition, my instinct — is broken. I was born with a faulty model that I've been trying to kill off for two decades. The medication helped for a while. Until it didn't. Until the shortage. Until there was no other alternative to sorrow except to build a new reality from the ground up with Adeline.

My mind whirs with the reality of this moment — was killing my husband a crime of passion? It's a crime of passion when a woman finds out her husband is cheating on her — but what if there was no affair — only evidence of one? And what if, left to the perceptions of a broken brain, the urge feels like a crime of passion but is more a crime perpetrated by mental illness?

Whatever the reality is, one thing is true: Albertine will be taken from me.

The court system will deem me no longer capable of being her mother, of raising the baby that lived inside of me for nine months.

I can't have that.

I will not lose someone else I love.

I cannot live with the reality that I killed my husband because I assumed he was cheating with the au pair. The au pair that has always been a vivid figment of my imagination. The realization that the day Adeline called the ambulance when Laurent had sunstroke wasn't real disturbs me on the deepest level.

I think then how easy it's been to pass off the lie that Alexandre left me for the au pair in a community like ours. It's funny what money can do in a place like this. People like to think that money means *more* investigating, but here, it means sweeping scandals under the rug.

I realize Marissa was right that day at the market months ago: in Palm Beach, *everyone* has a secret.

CHAPTER FORTY

"Ooh . . ." Albertine launches herself on the Italian leather sofa and presses her hands to the windows. "Pretty lights."

I finish wiping down the counter, fold the towel and hang it over the range. "What lights, baby?"

"Ooh a policeman is here!" She leaps off the couch and runs to the front door. "Can I open the door? He's a good guy, right?"

My blood turns to ice. My hands shake and I have to shove them in the pockets of my white chinos or I'll lose my ever-loving mind. "Sure, sweetie. You can open the door—" I come up behind her, "but don't let them in, okay?"

"Why not?" She inquires, hand hovering on the doorknob.

"Unannounced visitors aren't polite, that's why," I say swiftly.

Albertine slides the door open just as two uniformed officers are about to knock. The woman, younger with warm brown eyes and a tight bun, smiles at Albertine and then meets my eyes. "Genevieve Moreau-DuPont?"

I swallow the lump of pain in my throat and force a smile. "Yes."

"Is your husband Alexandre Moreau-DuPont?"

"Yes," I affirm.

"That's my daddy!" Albertine claps.

The woman smiles at Albertine and then addresses me again, "Is your husband home?"

"No, I'm afraid he's not," I state.

"Do you know when he will be home?" she asks.

I clear my voice, glancing down at my little girl. "I don't."

"Do you know where we could find him?"

"I do not," I admit.

The policeman pulls out a small notepad and writes something down. I try to catch a glimpse but his quick chicken scratch is too messy to make out. "How do you not know where your husband is?"

My face falls at his direct question. "Excuse me?" He only arches an eyebrow back at me. "What is this about exactly?"

"We got a call, Ms." The woman begins. "From your husband's workplace — he did work at Lawrence and Krauly Architects, right?"

It's not lost on me that she's just used the past tense — as if she already knows he doesn't work there anymore. As if she knows he never will again. I bite down on my bottom lip, wiping at emotion forming in my eyes. "He did." I glance down at Albertine. "If you don't mind, I'd rather not talk about what happened in front of my daughter."

Surprise covers the man's face while the woman nods warmly. She gets it, backing away a few steps and gesturing for me to come with her. I follow a few steps while Albertine looks up at the policeman and asks if he's carrying a gun. He indulges her with a smile and then bends and says something to her that I can't quite make out.

"What happened between you and your husband, Mrs. Moreau-DuPont?"

I push a hand over my face in a display of grief before I let a few stubborn tears fall. "He—" I sob, "he left with the help."

"He *what?*" She says, gaze narrowing.

"I hired an au pair a while back and I guess . . ." I whisper, "they knew each other. They were having an affair right under my nose—" I break with inconsolable tears.

The policewoman frowns and finishes writing something in her notepad before closing it and tucking it into her pocket. "Can we get her name?"

I sob and nod. "I–I think I have something with her name on it. I just — I feel like it's my fault because I didn't do a good job checking her references and I was just so desperate for help—"

"It's okay, Ms. If you find anything you think could be of use to us in finding him—"

"Is he in trouble or something?"

"No, no." She sends me a grin. "His firm called because he hasn't been into work and he hasn't called. Seems odd but I have to tell you, people disappear all the time looking for a new life. The grass is always greener, right?" She huffs as if she knows this well. "Anyway, we'll do what we can to find him but . . . forgive me for saying but maybe you don't want to know even if we do find him? If things are rocky between you two . . ."

A fresh wave of tears burns hot tracks down my cheeks. "I just need to move on from the trauma of infidelity — I can't stay in this house knowing they probably . . . were intimate everywhere. Everything feels like a betrayal."

"I thought so." Sympathy crosses the woman's face. "Officer Klein suspected foul play — a successful man just doesn't vanish like that, he said — but he's a new transfer. Maybe that stuff happens in Miami but in Palm Beach . . . well, a man that disappears here likely doesn't want to be found. All the iron-clad prenups in these gated communities have these fancy married people resorting to all kinds of ways of wiggling out of the financial obligation, ya know?" The woman chuckles. "Can you imagine? A murder in Palm Beach — things like that just don't happen in places like this."

I have to suppress a chuckle because clearly things like that *do* happen in places like this, only in places like Palm Beach, crimes are covered up to keep soaring real estate prices high. In fact, in places like this, law enforcement seems less on the side of the law and more on the side of maintaining the status quo for the top one per cent.

"I'd still feel more comfortable if we could take a little look around. You understand," the policeman's grin is tight. I don't trust him. And I guess he shouldn't trust me either. "Whaddya say you take me and Officer Barton here on a little tour of your house? Doesn't that sound fun?" The policeman is addressing Albertine specifically and it makes my blood boil.

"I'm afraid we don't really have time for that — this is a big house, a tour would take an hour at least and we have to get Albertine to her—" I falter, unable to think of an excuse on the fly.

"Actually, we don't need to see anything," the policewoman's warm eyes hover on mine. She understands. Woman to woman. She gets it. "We have to get back to the station anyway, the captain wants a few of us in uniform at the law enforcement gala tonight, remember?" She addresses her partner.

He arches an eyebrow, frown deepening.

"Oh — we donate to that charity!" I interject with a sweet smile.

"That's great! Glad to hear we have your support, Ms. Well," the policewoman begins to back away, "thanks for talking with us." She nods at her partner that she's finished. "We really appreciate your time."

Her partner stands, presses a sticker into Albertine's hands that looks like a police badge, and then pats her on the head. "Be a good girl for your mama, little lady."

"I will." Albertine beams and waves.

The man pauses and looks over Albertine's shoulder and into the house. "Is that bleach I smell?"

My heart stops. "I—" I slide an arm around Albertine's tiny shoulders, "we've been cleaning and donating some things to the local mission. Albertine has been learning about charity work at her school—" I lower my voice so Albertine can't hear, "I also have an appointment with a realtor in the morning, I just . . . don't think I can bear to stay in this house anymore." I let a few tears fall. "Too many painful memories."

The policewoman nods, then pulls a card from her pocket. "You call me if there's anything I can do, okay?"

193

The man still seems suspicious, eyes still trained inside my house. He inhales once, eyes flicking around as if he's mentally categorizing everything. I guide Albertine back into the house with me, a reassuring smile plastered on my face.

"Thank you." I wave at the officers and slide the front door closed. A wave of relief overcomes me as I lock the deadbolt and release a breath I didn't know I was holding.

We're safe. *For now.*

EPILOGUE

"Mommy!" Albertine screams, running through the house at full speed two weeks later.

"Yeah, baby?" I hum, my mind anywhere but on her. I lift the string of pearls that Alex gave me on our two-year wedding anniversary and clasp them behind my neck. They're still my favorite gift from him, even if it is hard, knowing how it all played out in the end.

"Are we moving yet?" Albertine's eyes are wide and hopeful.

"Give me just a few minutes and then we'll be on our way, okay?" I shuffle paperwork and stacks of old blueprints from Alex's office drawer. The house is sparse. From the main floor to the patio and bedrooms upstairs, it's been stripped clean of our life. As if we were never here; like our time in Palm Beach never existed.

I shove a stack of loose business papers in my tote bag but one falls out, fluttering to the floor. I bend, prepared to shove it back in my bag and be on my way with Albertine when I recognize it.

It's a letter to Alex. *From me.*

Heat swims in my stomach. I have the overwhelming urge to throw up.

I know what this letter is. And now I know that who it was meant for never received it because the envelope is still sealed. I wrote this letter the night before Laurent's funeral. The night before I met Adeline I poured my heart onto these bleached white pages and then tucked them into an envelope and placed it on a stack of my husband's blueprints in his office. Often when we wrote letters I left mine for him on his desk in his office and he left his letters for me in the hallway in the basket where I keep my car keys. A swell of regret consumes me as I realize Adeline must have found this on her first day here while she was cleaning up. She must have found it and shoved it with a stack of his work papers deep in his desk drawer, never to be found again.

Until now. By *me*.

I unfold the crisp pages and begin reading my familiar, tightly-clipped handwriting.

My Alex . . .

Something weird is happening. Everything is worse. I feel myself splitting into different perspectives, like my mind is wearing out and unraveling, shifting between them until their rough edges become defined lines. Until they are a part of me, co-existing, making decisions and . . . hurting us.

There's only one of me. It's all I've got. I hate seeing myself dissolve and slip and separate so that I'm living in one half watching as the other half of me is helpless and frantic and I can't stop it. Time is so long in these moments that even a second goes on and on.

I don't trust myself so I'm begging you, if anything strange happens please don't hesitate to call Dr. Valor at Pine Rest Psychiatric. He'll know what to do, he always does.

Please, if you notice anything strange, do something. Help. Don't wait. Sometimes a split-second decision is still a second too late.

Your Sugar

Waves of searing pain twist my insides.

Could all of this have been prevented if Alex had only found the letter? Alex and I used to write letters to each other all the time, if he'd found it, I know he'd read it instantly. That means he didn't find it — we never had a shot. *Adeline* made sure of it. Emotions swim behind my eyelids as I realize how much damage I've caused — how undeserving anyone is of this heartache.

Alex has never seen this side of me. In the six years since we've been married I learned to hide the slow unraveling of my mind well. Alex wouldn't know to recognize the signs because I didn't want him to. For a while he soothed the searing edges of my mind. I think back on one of the counselors I saw briefly before Alex and I met — she warned me that ruminating is the brain's way of attempting to fix the trauma, to right the wrongs, only it works in reverse — it causes the brain to relive the trauma, even growing it until the sheer size of the pain is bigger than it ever was to begin with.

I used to think dreams keep people from going crazy. Fantastical delusions that shelter our minds from the heartbreak of reality . . . but now, now I think dreams are a death sentence. I grew up feeling suffocated by the small-town drama of Pahokee, but it's just as easy to suffocate in Palm Beach too. Alex settled the turbulent seas of my heart and made me believe in fairytales.

For a while anyway.

I swallow down the tears welling up inside of me. I thought escaping the prison of my upbringing would set me free, but I know now that I'll never be free. The dreams of leaving my past behind are only illusions meant to plant seeds of hope in a barren wasteland. I realize now that wherever I go, I'll only find myself and the same hell I've always been running away from. Escape is a mirage. The real horror is in my mind.

Maybe that's just how it goes. You never know what you really want until you see it clearly.

No matter what happened, it was always going to be my fault, I think. But then Adeline, the ever-present devil lingering on my shoulder, pops into my head: *You probably just like thinking it was your fault.*

Fear and guilt are sisters. Identity and madness are a powerful cocktail until one is no longer separate from the other. Silent bitterness and an ocean of hurt permeated the air in our home, lingering long until it filled the cracks like spackle, impossible to root out. I was so strung out on despair that escape into the darkness was vital. And cloaked in regrets, Alex and I walked along together, gathering all of our fury and falling apart a little at a time.

I squint away tears, tucking the letter into my tote bag. Ruminating on what was won't do me any good. I've read enough self-help books to know that. Grief lurks like a painful monster at my door constantly begging for my attention these days, so now, I've built a room for it in my heart. *Learn to live with it or drown in it*, Adeline chimes. I take a breath, locking her in the basement of my mind where she belongs.

The human mind is powerful. Like alchemy, it can change reality and alter the future. Turn pain into peace and hate into love. I'm proof of that. One deftly planned step at a time I went from Pahokee to the penthouse. Growing, evolving, and becoming allows you to live different lives, leveling up and experiencing a new reality with a little grit and tenacity. I've always believed in burning my former life to the ground in the service of starting a new one. Rising from the ashes like a fucking phoenix is what I do best. The mind is full of shadows. The body contains our past emotions. I've learned we can't outrun either so I've dedicated my life to making lemonade out of rotten lemons.

"Mommy!" Albertine bounces up to me when I reach the bottom of the staircase. She wraps her arms around my legs in a tight hug. "Is it time to leave?"

"It is, baby." We walk out of the front doors and I swing the back door of the Audi open and Albertine climbs in, settling herself in her booster seat before I pull the seat belt around her shoulders. I tuck a lock of hair behind her ear and smile. "Are you ready for our next adventure?"

Her smile is broad and her cheeks are rosy with excitement. "Yeah!" She claps her hands. "Will Daddy meet us there?"

"Hopefully." I plant a kiss on her forehead and then close the back door and settle myself behind the wheel, fastening my seatbelt. I sigh, thoughts still swirling on Albertine's innocent question. I haven't had the heart to tell her that her daddy won't ever be coming back. Not for any nefarious reason other than I don't know *how* just yet.

For the sake of consistency, it'll be best if I run with the *he left with the help* lie for a lifetime. And when the time is right, I guess I'll tell her that.

My gaze crawls across the wide expanse of porch flanked with stately white pillars and a glossy black door. My dream home turned prison. I'd be lying if I didn't say I have some regrets, but it'll be hard to move on if I cling to them. Emotion threatens to crawl out of me when my vision tunnels to the inland waterway that weaves around the back of the estate.

I blink away a flashback.

Wrapping the wool rug around Alex's bloody body.

Lugging all two hundred pounds of him across the patio while Albertine watches movies locked safely in her playroom.

Past the pool. Out the gate. Down the path. Into the water.

Splashing. Saltwater. Tears.

I bite away the pain of Alex's watery grave. I can't help wondering if one step, even one minute had been different, would everything be different today? If the pharmacist had my refills when they should have, would I be sitting in my driveway crying over the loss of my daughter's father? The love of my life? The only man that made me feel like enough? If Alex had read the letter before and called Dr. Valor . . .

I swallow down the swirling thoughts and think that in the end none of it matters. All we ever have is this moment to make the best of. Alex was innocent, but weren't we all at one time? It was him or me — and when I woke up that morning and found him dead his fate was already sealed. I had to make a split decision and when the decision boiled down to getting justice for Alex's murder would also mean sending Albertine into the foster care system at the tender age of five . . . well, in the end there was no choice to be made. In the end it wasn't a matter of him or me. It was a matter of *her*.

I chose her. I'm still choosing her. She is the center of my universe and I will always choose her like nobody chose me . . . until Alex.

My stomach turns with quiet grief. I miss him the most in the quiet moments. I wish things could have been different for us.

I exhale a heavy sigh. "Well, all we can do is let go, and let God."

"What Mommy?" Albertine chimes from the backseat.

A tender smile lifts my lips. "I'm just sending a little prayer up to the universe for us, baby."

I let my eyes linger for a few more moments on the waterway behind our dream house, thinking Alex was a man deserving of more than just a brackish, watery burial. It doesn't matter though, with the frenzy of mating season underway, the alligators will have already cleaned up the mess I couldn't. The cycle of life at work, I guess.

I flip down the visor and purse my lips in the mirror before sliding a shiny Chanel gloss on top. I smile, thinking I should probably schedule a Botox appointment when we get to Naples. I adjust the pearls from Alex at my neck, smiling sweetly at the memory before my eyes land on a few flecks of crimson.

Blood.

"Hm." I frown, licking the pad of my thumb and then sliding it over the few scarlet-stained pearls until they're an iridescent milky white again. "There we go." I purse my lips one more time and then catch Albertine's intense brown eyes in the rearview mirror. *Alex's eyes.* My heart stirs painfully but I push the feeling away. Albertine watches me as if she knows what I've done. As if she can see the darkness that lingers in my soul, impossible to root out.

"Okay—" I break her piercing gaze, "it's you and me against the world now. What do you say to that?" I affect bright cheer for her sake.

"Girl power!" She strikes her little fist into the air and giggles.

And with death dripping from my pearls, I shift the Audi into reverse and grin. "I like that. To us and all we can become."

THE END

ACKNOWLEDGMENTS

My eternal gratitude goes to the team at Joffe Publishing for supporting my words, championing my twisty little stories, making this book the very best it could be, and getting it into more readers' hands. You're in the business of making dreams come true and always such a pleasure to work with.

Thank you to my counselor for letting me cry out decades of trauma on her couch and pushing me to build community . . . you're a lifesaver and have helped me become the woman I was meant to be.

For those struggling with mental illness: you are loved, and sometimes all it takes is a tender, listening ear and a hug from a friend to turn someone's day around.

Thank you to the men showing up with respect and raising sons that know how to love. The world needs more of you.

To my readers: thank you for spending time with my twisted stories. If you send an email to info@adrianeleigh. com, I will personally respond. You can also find a list of book signings and events I'm attending, and keep up with my latest releases by visiting adrianeleigh.com. I love to talk all things books and make new book friends! Your support means more than words can express. From the bottom of my heart, thank you.

If you or someone you love needs mental health support, please reach out:

US: The National Mental
Health Hotline: +01 866 903 3787

UK: Mind Support Line: +44 0300 102 1234

Australia: Beyond Blue
Support Line: +61 1300 224 636

THE JOFFE BOOKS STORY

We began in 2014 when Jasper agreed to publish his mum's much-rejected romance novel and it became a bestseller.

Since then we've grown into the largest independent publisher in the UK. We're extremely proud to publish some of the very best writers in the world, including Joy Ellis, Faith Martin, Caro Ramsay, Helen Forrester, Simon Brett and Robert Goddard. Everyone at Joffe Books loves reading and we never forget that it all begins with the magic of an author telling a story.

We are proud to publish talented first-time authors, as well as established writers whose books we love introducing to a new generation of readers.

We won Trade Publisher of the Year at the Independent Publishing Awards in 2023 and Best Publisher Award in 2024 at the People's Book Prize. We have been shortlisted for Independent Publisher of the Year at the British Book Awards for the last five years, and were shortlisted for the Diversity and Inclusivity Award at the 2022 Independent Publishing Awards. In 2023 we were shortlisted for Publisher of the Year at the RNA Industry Awards, and in 2024 we were shortlisted at the CWA Daggers for the Best Crime and Mystery Publisher.

We built this company with your help, and we love to hear from you, so please email us about absolutely anything bookish at feedback@joffebooks.com.

If you want to receive free books every Friday and hear about all our new releases, join our mailing list here: www.joffebooks.com/freebooks.